THE GIRL ON THE BRIDGE

She didn't move, and he couldn't either until he saw her lean out further and raise an arm.

"Hello! You—"

He didn't catch the question in her voice, he acted only by instinct, yanked out the gun and aimed it up.

"You, down there—" he heard again, but not the rest. As he turned, the pain in his side boiled over, twisted the girl on the bridge out of focus. For a moment he felt as if he had to throw up, and he became so weak he could barely balance himself. He gasped, rested, holding on to the bank.

When his strength came back it came slowly, from the brain, so he knew what he had to do. Because if he stopped now, it meant that he would have to run forever.

The rage crawled through him like a flush, slow and hot, and he started up the embankment, probing the gun in his hand ahead of him.

She stood motionless in the half light, her hair spilling around her face. As long as she didn't move it was like a spell on him and he started to kill her every step of the way. He didn't rush her; he stalked. Every step of the way—until she moved.

"Hello," she said. "Are you sick?"

PETER RABE

A HOUSE IN NAPLES

PASAPORTE

WILDSIDE PRESS

To
HAL CANTOR
my thanks.

A HOUSE
IN NAPLES

Chapter One

THE WARM PALM of land cupped the water to make a
bay, and that's where Naples was.

He stood high up watching the view run down the side
of the hill. Then he pushed away from the garden wall
and walked again. He was in the outskirts where Naples
was like a village, quiet because the day had just started.
When he came to the square he stopped again. It had a
downhill tilt and he tried not to look at it but focused
on the opposite street. He wiped one hand across his face.
The tanned skin was moist and the sun made his cheekbones shine. He crossed slowly and on the other side he
stopped again. Leaning against the cold stone wall along
the small street he looked like a man who had a lot of
time. His face was in shadow now and didn't look so
sharp any more. The high cheekbones were without the
sharp lines and he relaxed his mouth. There was a curve
to it, like a smile. It was there whether he smiled or not.

A young woman turned into the street. She carried a
bundle on top of her head and he watched how her big
peasant skirt made swirls when she walked.

"*Buon giorno*, Charley," she said, and the way she pro-
nounced it the name sounded Italian.

He said *buon giorno* and nodded. Then he walked again.
When the street dipped a little he saw the steps leading
up to the white house. First the steps went one way, twelve
of them, then came the landing and the steps went the
other way, thirteen of them. Most of the house was behind unkempt bushes.

7

After the first twelve steps he stopped on the landing without looking down at the view. Thirteen more steps. He grabbed the stone ramp hard and walked. Where he had left the landing the flagstone had five spots. The blood was dark and thick.

After a while he made the top. He walked through the disordered garden, found the side entrance. The wooden door stood open and he walked into the kitchen. The low room was cool stucco and looked dark after the sun.

A pine table stood in the middle and Joe Lenken sat there the way he always sat. His big arms lay on the table.

"Kinda early for visiting," he said. He looked sullen, not caring how he sounded.

"How come you're up?" Charley looked at Joe behind the table, then at the dark girl who stood by the cold hearth. There was a hot plate on the hearth and the girl was dumping a can of tomato soup into the pot.

"I woke up," said Joe.

Charley kept standing, not wanting to sit because he thought maybe he'd stumble if he took another step. He had his hands in his pockets. It made his seersuckers look like a bag.

"A new one?" said Charley and nodded at the girl.

"Ya."

She came up with the warm tomato soup and put it down in front of Joe. She was young. It was hard to tell just how young she was because her body was all filled out, but the face looked like a dumb child.

"She speak English?"

"A little."

"Tell her to get me some aspirin," Charley said, and then he blinked because sweat had run into his eye. He wiped his forehead and it made the hair moist. Cut short, it stood out like feathers, colored dusty, because he had a funny mixture of red-brown and white hair.

The girl brought aspirin in a box and a glass of water. Charley took four pills, put them behind his lip, didn't take the water. He sucked the sharp pills, waiting for the sting to run down his throat, and then he held on to the back of the chair and sat down.

"You sick?" Joe was slurping soup. His thick face was red from the sun because he had the kind of complexion that never tanned. He licked his lip where some soup was and then he asked again. "You sick or something?"

The aspirin was an Italian kind and very cheap. Charley liked them best because they took so long to dissolve.

"I got shot," he said. "Over the hip."

"That why you come busting in here at dawn?"

"I couldn't make it to my place." Charley was sweating again. "The ball's still in there, I think."

"Stupid bastard."

"My buddy," said Charley. His foot came up slow and he kicked his end of the table. It slopped Joe's soup. "Take it out, Joe. Like a buddy, huh?" and this time he kicked the table so the bowl jumped to the floor.

Joe got up. He didn't wipe the soup off his pants, just got up and left the kitchen. He said "stupid bastard" once more. When he came back he had a carton with bottles and bandages. There were some instruments too.

"Get on the table," he said and sorted out the stuff in his box.

Charley got on the table and groaned.

"Take the pants off."

"You gotta give me a hand."

"Fanny," said Joe. "Take 'em off."

Her name was Francesca, but that was too much to pronounce for Joe Lenken.

"I guess it's all right," said Charley. "Seeing you're in the room."

"What a clown," said Joe, and while Francesca pulled Charley's pants off Joe poured alcohol over some instruments in a dish. Francesca took the pants, the shorts, and then she came back to look at the wound. It was a red hole in the flesh over the hip and there was blood all the way down the leg.

"She's a real trouper," said Charley. He felt sweaty and sick but he had to say something so it wouldn't feel worse. "How'd she get that way, Joe buddy? You didn't have her when I left. Just a week ago."

"I learn 'em fast," said Joe. He washed alcohol over his hands and rubbed them. "Wanna shot before I start?"

"Go to hell," said Charley.

Joe laughed because this was his kind of joke. Charley never took whisky. It made him sick.

"So be brave," said Joe and then he went to work.

Charley fainted right off which was a good thing because his buddy Joe didn't give a damn one way or the other.

Chapter Two

BECAUSE HIS SIDE FELT SORE he got out of bed with a slow roll. When he stood it wasn't so bad. Francesca had washed his clothes and he put them on, leaving the belt loose. First he went and shaved, then he walked through the low door into the kitchen. Joe Lenken was there, at the table like before, and if there had been any spots on the white pine top Francesca had scrubbed them clean. She was standing next to Joe's chair and his arm was around her hip. Joe turned his head.

"You been out all day," said Joe.

Charley could tell by the sun. The light outside wasn't morning any more. It shone red through the leaves outside the door and made the kitchen look darker.

"Farmer Joe and his sturdy woman enjoying the vesper hour," said Charley. He walked to the other end of the table and sat down. "I see real bliss there," he said. "After an active day in the hot sun, Farmer Joe having some quiet frolic with his woman at the kitchen table."

Joe didn't say anything. He didn't know what vesper hour meant and didn't give a damn. His arm stayed around the girl who leaned against him like a farm animal.

"What happened to the last one?" said Charley. "Wouldn't hold still long enough?" The curve of his mouth was like a smile.

"She was getting too old," said Joe.

"That figures. You had her a whole month."

Charley pulled the aspirin out of his pocket and took two pills. He put them under his tongue and watched Joe.

"Stop pawing a minute. We got business."

"Make you nervous?"

"Ya. She might wake up and then what?"

Joe laughed and kept his arm there. He had a laugh like a rock jumping down a hillside, only it never got any faster and then it stopped.

"I know all about it. You lost the whole truckload."

10

"Who told you?"

"Vittore was here. He said they ambushed the truck like you wanted to give it to them."

"Vittore didn't say that. He wasn't around long enough to tell."

"I say it."

Lenken had his hand on the girl's hip and Charley moved the pills inside his mouth. Then Charley said, "You made the arrangements, clinker head. They got a thousand gallons of gasoline. There were enough *carabinièri* in those woods to stop a convoy."

"Maybe you're saying I sent 'em?"

"No, but you might just as well. You didn't check out that greedy bastard enough, that creep who sold us the stuff."

"He delivered. You lost it."

"Sure. He highjacked the gas in Trieste where they watch every ship that docks like it had bombs on it. He left a trail—"

"He never goofed before."

"That was small time. They don't watch so hard when Swiss watches get lost, or some nylon."

"Have it your way, Chuck. The creep goofed, I goofed, but not you. You just lose the stuff and get yourself shot."

"Lenken, stop pawing that girl a minute."

"Beat it, Chuck, willya? And next time you handle the works. You're the brains; you handle it."

Charley had the pill box in his hand and started to rattle it back and forth.

"Maybe there won't be a next time."

"Sure," said Lenken.

"Send out the girl."

"Ten years in the black market and never a hitch. Maybe a loss here and there, so what. But then Chuck boy gets shot in the skin, there's blood, and right away there's a catastrophe." Lenken shifted his weight. "You're scared, Chuck."

"You're right."

Charley paused because he saw that Joe was listening now. Joe closed his mouth, then opened it. The way he let it hang gave him a stupid look except that Charley knew better. Joe wasn't stupid and Joe wasn't exactly slow. He'd heard about that ambush even before Charley walked into the kitchen. He didn't rant, didn't complain about the

loss, didn't apologize because the mess was mostly his fault.
He didn't even hide the way he felt, that maybe one
more fluke like that and Charley might not be around to
tell about it.

Joe must be thinking it was time to let their combine go
to pieces. He didn't need Charley any more. Ten years ago
he did. He needed Charley because Charley had the brains
and Joe had just the cunning. He needed Charley because all that Joe was good at were details. They'd gotten
in the racket while the Occupation was still on, when
things were easy. They made a team and stayed in
the black market ever since. They didn't get into each
other's way because they never tried too hard to make
a friendship out of it. They didn't have to. What kept
them close was quite something else.

"So grin a little harder," said Joe. "Maybe the scare
will go away."

"Send out the girl."

"Make you nervous?"

"Send her out, Corporal."

Joe stopped with his hand. He gave the girl a push,
told her to beat it. Then he put both arms on the table
and talked low.

"Chuck. I don't want you to say that."

Charley smiled and started to rattle his pills again.
"Now that you're listening—"

"Don't say that again, Chuck."

"Joe," said Charley, "it's better I say it than somebody else."

Joe got up and hitched his pants. The girl was still
in the kitchen, at the far end. She was standing there
with nothing to do. Joe yelled at her in Italian and
watched her run out the door. Then he came around the
table.

"Listen here," he said, and looked down at Charley.
"What's eating you?"

"Trouble," said Charley.

Joe sucked his teeth and looked out the door where the
red sun was almost gone. Then he looked back at Charley,
only nothing showed. The bastard looked like he was smiling. He'd smile if he were killing his grandmother, thought
Joe. That smile used to confuse him, until he found out
that you couldn't go by Charley's face. You could always
go by what Charley said, though. When Charley said

trouble it was trouble, and when he said fine things were fine.

"Let's go to the *osteria*," said Charley and when he walked out the door Joe just followed.

They went down the street, crossed the square, and went uphill a little. Couples were making the circle around the square and old people sat in the small gardens. Somebody greeted them now and then. Charley waved back, but Joe didn't answer.

They came to the *osteria*, and since they owned the place they went to the back, down the stairs, and into the basement room which had a fancy cylinder lock on the door. Except for the cylinder lock it wasn't much of a room, and the trap door in the floor didn't show. That's where they kept the high-priced stuff, like German precision tools or the small boxes with hard-to-get medicines.

"Listen to that racket," said Charley and looked up at the ceiling. "Beats me how they get happy just on that coffee and vino."

Joe sat down and waited to hear about the trouble.

"Hear that music," said Charley. "That's old Silvestro making music. Every time it sounds like the espresso machine blowing its top, that'll be Silvestro singing a shepherd song."

"Let's hear it, Chuck."

"You will," and Charley sat down. He put his feet on the safe by the wall, a rusty and beat-up thing, but the mechanism inside was new. "That ambush was worse than just losing the merchandise. It—"

"Ya, I know. They fired guns and it scared you."

"Worse, Lenken. They got a good look at me. They caught me and in the headlights they got a good look at me."

That's when Joe sat back and didn't seem interested any more: "So maybe you'll get a couple of years," he said. "Good riddance."

For the first time Charley raised his voice. It was sharp and he talked fast.

"Not a couple of years, you dumb bastard. The rope! Or worse, you bastard. Maybe life!"

Joe knew what Charley meant but it didn't faze him. "You got a fever, Chuck?"

"I got a fever. I got a fever to stay the way I am,

stay left alone, stay so your and my uncle don't know
about it." And then his voice got so quiet Joe could
just hear it. "Or maybe you don't remember, Corporal.
You and me are deserters."

They didn't say anything for a while because everything was clear. If they got caught for jaywalking and the
police had nothing better to do for the moment and
started to look at papers, at dates and names on their
papers, then pretty soon the whole rotten underpinnings
would start to shake. Joe Lenkva, born Iowa, U.S.A.,
a farm boy with no skill except running potato tillers,
good stuff for the infantry, sturdy stuff all the way up
through Africa, making corporal in the motor corps because good stuff Lenkva was just the right type of noncom
material. They never suspected he had a brain of his
own. He always kept his mouth hanging open, which
made him look stupid. That's how cunning he was. He
didn't care how stupid he looked.

So when Lenkva hit Anzio he didn't run because he
was scared. He ran because he figured it was best that
way all around. And he made it. He made it from Corporal Lenkva to Joe Lenken, Italy, tavern owner and
lover of Fannys.

Or if they caught Charley driving a truck with the
wrong kind of merchandise in the back and they should
look at his papers a little too long, they would find he'd
been Charley all along, but the first time he changed his
last name was when he ran away from home. Home
wasn't much good, with too many brothers and sisters
and not enough mother and father. So he picked fruit for
a while and then the season was over. He washed dishes
in Frisco, got a good look at the bums on Mission Street,
but that was too much like home so he ran again. He
learned being a carpenter where the developments mush-
roomed in the valley next to Los Angeles and that was
all right until they got organized there. He had saved
his dough so he ran again. When he walked into the
little town at the foot of the Rockies he had another
name, just from habit. There wasn't any building going
on there so he started to pump gas for Old Benton, who
had the only station for miles around. Just when Charley
bought a piece of Old Benton's garage the draft caught
up with him and being a fast liar and the only available
male in town, Charley made private in nothing flat. He

stayed that way until Anzio and when it came to the point where the platoon was gone, all dead, Charley was still alive. That had been luck.

From there on it wasn't luck but determination, or at least luck used to his best advantage. Charley ran again. He ran good that time—so good he figured he'd never run again, not change his name again except this one time when he went underground—and watched the advantages. Victory made everybody generous, which was an advantage, and when Charley showed up again he was an American immigrant with an easy way about business, smiling most of the time because that's how his face was built. If he was worried or if he had eyes in the back of his head, it didn't show. Charley didn't drink in the afternoon and he didn't have a nervous smoking habit. All he did was eat aspirin, and few people knew about that.

Chapter Three

CHARLEY STOPPED RATTLING the aspirin box.

"If they look too hard we got a problem," he said.

"So run," said Joe.

It caught Charley by surprise, as if Joe was showing him the door but didn't think he was going to use it himself.

"So run," Joe said again.

Charley got up. When it stung him where the bandage was he hardly noticed.

"Run! I'm through running, you bastard! I'm sticking where I am because I like standing still for once, and I'm not doing you any favors and lam out of here pulling the chase after me. If they get me, Joe, they get you!"

"Not me, Chuck. With me everything's legit."

Charley sat down. He was grinning.

"Do tell. Like what, Joey? You going to marry little Fanny?" but Charley saw how the joke wasn't making any dent. When Joe folded his arms he suddenly looked even bigger than he was.

"It's like this, Chuck. They're not looking for me, and if they were they couldn't prove a thing. I been running the *osteria* and minding my own business at home. Right, Chuck?"

Charley nodded, kept listening.

"And if they get you, Chuck, you wouldn't drag me into it, would you, Chuck?"

"Don't get cute."

"So there's nobody after me in this country. I got Italian papers good as gold. Citizenship, Chuck. You didn't know that, did you, Chuck?"

Charley hadn't known that.

"Perhaps I look stupid, Chuck—"

"You do."

"—but I'm not."

"No, you're not."

"And I'll show you why. That Corporal Lenkva you keep talking about, let's say Uncle Sam is still looking for him. If they find him that means extradition. I can

16

fight extradition, Chuck, because the Italians would have
to arrest me—except they don't arrest peaceful çitizens
that got no record and just run a tavern up in the outskirts. And here's the payoff, Chuck. Uncle Sam's not
looking for me."

"Oh no. They just want you to have a good time with
Fanny and not bother about a little thing like a general
court martial for desertion."

Joe laughed and the sound bounced around for a while
without going up or down.

"That's the truth, Chuck. Remember that G.I. insurance? Well, it's been seven years and more, so if somebody wants to collect they can make a request after seven
years. The court declares me dead and they collect the
money. That's what my mother did. She went and had
me declared dead and collected the ten thousand. So now
it's even legit for Uncle Sam. I'm dead and nobody's
looking."

Charley thought about that and saw it was a neat set-
up. Joe hadn't wasted his time. He had played all the
angles. He was dead in the States and alive in Italy—
with papers to prove it. When Joe said they were good
as gold he must be sure they were. Joe had had ten years
to find himself the best—so did Charley, except he hadn't.
He'd been glad to be standing still, to buy a residence
permit once, a forged passport another time, and a birth
certificate that didn't match. He'd been standing still letting things drift, never worrying about details. But Joe,
the moron . . .

"Joe, that insurance deal. I got—"

"Who's your beneficiary, Chuck?"

"Old Benton. The old guy with the gas station."

Joe shook his head and crossed his arms the other way.
"No good, Chuck. You told me he'd died the year after
you left, and had no heirs except you. Whoever you
were then. And you never changed beneficiaries, did you,
Chuck?"

He hadn't. Just one of those things.

"Just one of those things, huh, Chuck? Uncle Sam figures you might be alive, the *carabinièri* know you are, and
you know you haven't got any papers. Messy, Chuck."

Messy. Smart boy Charley who'd been on his own ever
since he ran off from home, too smart to bother with details because details were for morons—he finally got it what

a clever moron Joe Lenken was and how stupid a smart guy could be. Like all the other times when he had started to run.

"How'd you get those papers, Joe? From Del Brocco?"

"Naw. Del Brocco's a forger. My papers are the real stuff I told you."

"All right, where'd you get them? Don't sit there like a lurch. You want this thing to blow wide open?"

"I told you, Chuck. I'm safe."

Charley came around to Joe's chair and bent down.

"Lenken, you're safe as long as I'm safe. So don't be coy with your Charley horse, Joe, because when I sink, you sink. Remember?"

"You'd drag me in?"

"No. But I wouldn't make an effort to keep you out. Now listen to me. They may never get to me and then again they might. I'm leaving for Rome to see Del Brocco. Meanwhile—"

Somebody tapped on the door.

"Joey, you in there?"

"Who wants to know?"

"Joey, it's me."

"Who in hell—"

"Marco. I got to see you, Joey."

"Talk through the door," said Charley.

"That you, Charley? I didn't know—"

"Now you do. And I'm fine. So talk."

"They got Vittore," said Marco. "The *carabinièri* just brought him into the *gendarmeria*. About a stolen truck."

Marco waited, but nobody said a word behind the door. And Charley waited, hoping there wouldn't be any more.

"That truck wasn't stolen," said Joe as if it was important.

Charley sucked air through his teeth and stepped to the door. "Okay, Marco. Beat it."

Marco's steps went away.

Charley hadn't moved but the change was there. He looked quiet because he was holding it just a moment longer, before the fast rush to save what he could, the run for his life.

"I'm going to Rome. While I'm gone make me an alibi. Vittore might hold out a couple of days, but you make me an alibi. Then—"

"Like what, Chuck?"

"Like it was for you. Make it good, Joe, and no mistake. I'll call you here every day, this hour. Keep your ears open and try to get Vittore out. Clear?"

It was clear to Joe he better not push Charley right then. Charley needed a name like he never did before, and this time when he started to run he meant it to be the last time. Joe saw him off that night. He watched Charley gun the motor of his Bugatti so it was good enough to jump clear across the bay.

"Addio," said Joe.

"I'll be back," said Charley and then he watched the road shoot by.

Chapter Four

DEL BROCCO WAS AN ARTIST. It meant he knew he was good, he kept no regular hours, and his prices were over the top. That was because his customers knew he was good. But Del Brocco lived in a part of Rome where the gutter was in the middle of the street and if you stood on a house balcony on either side you could drop things straight down and make the gutter.

Charley parked on a market square and walked the rest of the way. It was dark. There were no lights, no house numbers, but Del Brocco's house stood out. It had a seventeenth-century doorway which in itself meant little enough in that part of town. But his house was built of the biggest stones, going back to the time when they looted the Colosseum to build their dark little houses behind the walls of Rome.

When Charley tapped on the door nobody answered. After a while a girl opened the window across the street and leaned out. Even if Charley hadn't understood her Italian he would have known what she meant. He told her something so she closed the window and then he tapped again. He tapped three, two, one, three, which he should have remembered sooner and when the door opened, Del Brocco's sons were there. The short one was six feet and the tall one a lot more.

"Del Brocco. I'm Charley."

"He is not here."

"For me he is. Let me in."

"He is not here, *signore.*"

"Don't *signore* me. Tell Del Brocco—" They grabbed his arms, heaved at the same time, and Charley was where the gutter was.

If the fall hadn't made his side hurt like hell he might have done it differently, but he picked himself up slowly and walked to the grilled window in the front of the house. He hung his jacket on the grillwork, making it drape so it looked like something, and then he went back to the gutter. He brought back a stick and punched out all of Del Brocco's little leaded windows.

Six foot and six foot plus came out of the door like heroes taking a town singlehanded, and just about when they started to tangle with Charley's coat he walked through the door, banged it shut, and threw the bolt. Then he looked for Del Brocco.

Like the two boys had said, the house was empty. There were Del Brocco's antiques, his tapestries and expensive furniture, and his stamp collection was open on his desk. So Charley went back to the front room where the broken window was. He climbed on a carved chest, opened one side of the old window, and leaned against the grillework. "Hey," he said.

They ran up under the window and started to curse. After a while they stopped.

"Where's Del Brocco?" said Charley.

"He is gone, he left before you came, days ago, even a week, you—"

"When's he coming back?"

One of them kept cursing and the other one complained about the window. "The fifteenth-century window," he moaned, "the irreplaceable—"

"Shut up a minute."

When they did he leaned on the sill the way the girl had done it and tried again.

"About the window, boys, don't worry about it. Just think what might happen to the stuff inside here and nobody stopping me."

They held still and listened.

"When's he coming back?"

"One month and three days, *signore*."

"Ah yes. Those three days. And where is he?"

"In prison, *signore*."

That took care of Del Brocco. And Charley. He almost felt like breaking something else but he let it go.

"And who takes care of his customers in the meantime?"

"*Signore,* no one can take care of—"

"I know. But who else is there?"

"There is Alivar."

"Where?"

"The bookstore on the Via Claudia."

"And now if you'll hand me my jacket—shake it out a little. That's it—"

They handed it through the grillework and Charley put it on.

"When I come out, boys, I'll tell you about the window. Nothing to worry about. I'll explain," he said and got off the chest and went to the door. When he had it open they were waiting for him.

"Del Brocco told me," he said, "not to worry about the window. It's false, you know. The real one is up in the attic. Back where he keeps the dismantled altar."

They went past him to get to the attic, and Charley walked out. He didn't know about the window, though he had seen the altar up in the attic. He thought it might be nice if there were another window.

This time the street was wider, letting the moon shine down to the cobblestones. Alivar's little shop was one in a row. Alivar was asleep. After ringing the bell for a while Charley said *polizia* through the door and that got the old man up.

He wasn't so old, he only looked wrinkled with severe lines running down the side of his nose and cold eyes that never changed even when Charley told him about Del Brocco.

"You may speak English," said Alivar. "I myself am not an Italian."

"So you know how it is," said Charley.

When Alivar nodded, Charley wondered what he had understood. They went the length of the stalls, through a back room with more books and a canopied bed, and up to the second floor. It was a bare attic, without windows, and even though it was three in the morning the heat was thick under the roof. Alivar did not sweat.

"You need a name?"

"The works. Birth certificate, naturalization papers, driver's license, registration—money's no object."

"It is with me," said Alivar.

"With me it's only time."

"About one month," said Alivar.

"Too long. How about just a passport? An American passport."

Alivar laughed as if he were listening to a child. "Unobtainable," he said.

"Del Brocco could get me one."

"Yes. He is also in jail."

They argued a little longer, but it wasn't any good. Alivar went down to his canopied bed and for 20,000 lire Charley stayed in the attic and slept past daylight. Then the heat drove him out.

Charley started to make the rounds. With Del Brocco and Alivar he had run out of the high-class artisans. What came next were the defunct engravers, and when he ran out of those he saw the thieves who stole papers. In ten years' time he had heard of most of them, and spending this day was almost like another ten years. By noon he was limping with the pain in his side, but when he ran out of aspirin by three in the afternoon he still kept going. He was running for the last time, he had to have his name—one that stuck—even if it meant it would go only on his tombstone.

None of them were any good; cheap forgeries dolled up to be good enough for one quick look or stolen papers with a tracer on them since the minute they were lifted. It seemed to get worse by evening—everything, the heat, the rain, and the slipshod ware he was looking at. For once in his life he needed the real thing and while he kept running he kept telling himself it was going to be over soon and then he'd never run again. If he made it in time.

Chapter Five

Two thousand years ago Rome had a harbor, Ostia. Today Ostia is like Coney Island, with the same kind of fry odors, tinsel excitement, and brass sounds of all Coney Islands. It shuts down after a while, late at night, and only some places stay open. There is a ring of permanent buildings at the edges of Ostia, old and ratty, and that part of Rome doesn't have the excuse of real age, of being antique. It just stinks. There are rooming houses, some dives, and the usual *osterias*.

Charley sat in the crowded place and ate his *Piatto del Giorno*. It smelled more like fish than fish ought to. He looked at the packed bar, the tables that made an untidy clutter all over the room. There was a door to the corridor in the back and every so often somebody went there. It wasn't the toilet. The toilet was outside, in the rear.

Charley pushed his plate away and moved carefully in his chair, because of his side. It was nighttime, after a bad day. He still had no name. He sat and was still running. Maybe the way things were going he wouldn't need a new name. They'd dig up the old ones and then maybe they'd give him a number.

He ate an aspirin and ordered some coffee. The long bar was only a few feet away, but he had to yell for it because of the racket. He watched the girl wind herself his way with the cup and the pot but it took her a while. There were a lot of customers who weren't thinking of buying coffee when she came by and then a French sailor walked up and had a discussion with her. He put his duffle bag on Charley's table so there wasn't much room for anything else and then his buddy came up. While they were trying to convince the girl the buddy kept sipping from the coffee she was holding. She must have said the right thing after a while because they let her pass, the sailor picked up his duffle bag, gave Charley a friendly nod, and helped put the cup and pot on the table. They took the girl by one arm each and Charley didn't have to pay for his coffee.

The strong stuff burned his mouth, but that's what he wanted. Another hour before making his call, and then what? The way the pressure was building up it didn't matter much what the phone call would say. The phone call couldn't give him a month till Del Brocco got out of jail or till Alivar got around to fixing him up. It never occurred to him to hide for a month, to wait a month or more till he looked legal again. One way or another it had to be soon, and for good.

"Hey, buddy boy."

At first Charley didn't hear. He was breathing carefully because of his side and he wasn't going to make any fast movements because he felt it might end up a swing in somebody's face.

"Dear liddle buddy boy," said the voice again, and this time Charley couldn't ignore it. The smell was strong and the drunk dropped in the chair opposite.

"Don't feel so bad," said the drunk. His confidential manner was ugly. "She'll be back in maybe ten minutes, buddy boy, couldn't take longer, and you can order more coffee."

"Who asked you?"

"Who cares," said the drunk, "as long as you're listening." His worn-out face made a squint and leaned closer. "And when she's back we're next. Them French may look hot, buddy boy, but they don't last but a minute. Like rabbits, get it?" He laughed with his teeth showing. He didn't have too many.

Charley sipped coffee and looked quiet. He even had the small smile around his mouth. Let the drunk talk and maybe the time will pass faster.

"And when she comes back we'll show her what's what, huh, buddy boy?"

"All you ever got stiff on is a bottle," said Charley and looked friendly.

It made a pause. The drunk worked his tongue around one tooth and looked at Charley like murder.

"You trying to beat my play?" he said. "I saw her first. I been sitting here all afternoon before you ever showed up, buddy boy, and I been watching her all that time."

"That figures."

"You American, ain'tcha?"

Charley didn't answer.

"So am I. That's why I figured I give you a break, buddy. That's the only reason I figured—"

"Don't put yourself out."

The drunk reached a bottle out of his coat and sucked. It wasn't just any old hooch, but rye with an American label. That drunk had connections.

"Notice that bottle?" he said. "I ain't been in the States for twenty years, buddy boy, but I know my way around." He watched for Charley to look impressed but Charley only smiled.

"Twenty years on one bottle. You're doing real good."

The drunk answered something but Charley wasn't listening. He looked at his watch, checking time, and thought the drunk hadn't turned out to be the funny kind.

"—high-hat a countryman, you sonofabitch," the drunk was saying. He sounded vicious. "Maybe you're one of them slumming tourists coming around here, having fun with the local color? I'll give you color, you damn son-ofa—" and the drunk hauled out with his bottle.

It didn't take much to grab the bottle away from him and push him back in his chair. But Charley was getting irritated. The time was grating him, his side hurt like hell, and he had to sit without getting anything done. He was dying for aspirin. The drunk reached for his bottle but Charley knocked his hand out of the way.

"Behave, bum. Or I'll have you deported."

It made the drunk laugh till his pale scalp turned red.

"Deported, he says! Deported where, Officer? To hell, maybe? I been there. To the U.S.? I can't get a visa. Or maybe back where I come from just a few days ago? Oh, wouldn't they love that back there. A guy pays my way all the way back like I never been gone and oboyoboy—" he ended up gurgling and reached for the bottle again.

Charley let him. He watched the wrinkled neck with the Adam's apple jerking around and then he wiped his hands. Fifteen minutes till the call, and then run again. Back to Alivar, maybe, but first a few other stops. He had to swing it one way or another—

"You can't deport me," the drunk was saying. He sounded off-hand, made an important gesture. "On account of the people I know. Besides, I'm an Italian. Been that ever since Thirty-five. Boy, those were the days. Ever hear of Benny?"

"Sure. Big wheel at the Last Chance Mission."

"Listen, you sonofabitch. Benito. I mean Benito."

"Oh, sure. You're the one arranged for the Abyssinian War."

"Those were the days," said the drunk. His eyes were up and he thought about those days. "Whaddaya mean, war?" He came back to earth, looking mean. "I was at the reception. Two of 'em! Benny's buddy, one of his buddies was renting my villa on Ischia so that's how we were pals. And I got to go to all the receptions, tourist! Me!"

"So what happened to Benny?"

"Who cares about Benny. Listen, tourist, I don't need nobody. I got my own life, nobody tells me nothing, and I go where I please." The drunk leaned his chin in one hand and looked coy. "Bet you don't know where I was two days ago?"

"Did they have polka-dot elephants there?"

"Listen, tourist. Don't talk. I was in Cairo, buddy boy. Five years in Cairo!"

"That's big stuff. Real big stuff."

"I hope to tell you," said the drunk, and tilted the bottle. "And how did I get back?"

"By boat."

"Right! And me, Delmont, I come and go with nobody telling me nothing. What a joke!" he laughed. "What a joke!"

"What joke?"

"Five years in Cairo, tourist, and me with no papers! All that time they're lying here in my trunk, safe as safe, and me without papers. That's operating!"

"I'll say. So they threw you out. That's real operating."

"Who, the police?" and he gurgled his laugh again. "Listen, tourist, my buddy Amir brung me back, on his little yacht. I come back the way I left, nobody the wiser. That's how I operate!"

"Good old Amir," said Charley, but it sounded mechanical. He had enough of the game. It was time to phone.

"Amir is a sonofabitch," said the drunk, "another of you high-hat sonsabitches, only Egyptian. After five years he throws me out, me, Delmont, what showed him how to operate. Listen, tourist, that lurch is no friend of mine. I only got one buddy. Me. And Bantam, maybe."

Bantam. Charley knew of a Bantam.

"My buddy Bantam. I gotta go see him tomorrow maybe. Ten years is a long time for buddies to be apart; maybe my buddy—"

The drunk was getting whiney and Charley saw it was time. He didn't listen any more because the drunk had done his job. Time was up. Call Joe. Charley squeezed to the bar and said he wanted a phone. He went through the curtain in back, found the door with light behind it and went in. There was a phone on the beat-up desk and a guy sleeping on a couch. Charley got Naples.

"Joe?"

"Ya. I'm here."

"Look, Joe, it isn't good. It'll be a while, unless I dig something up between now and tomorrow. The merchandise I want is scarce."

"I know. You shoulda done like I done. Start early and take your time."

"Don't preach, dammit. Now look, I'll be back tomorrow late, because—"

"That's too early, Chuck."

"What?"

"Hell broke loose."

"What are you talking about! Vittore lose his head?"

"He just talked."

"Oh that everloving bastard! What—"

"They been here, looking for you. They figured I knew something, seeing Vittore hangs around our place. They're around asking for Charley. You."

"That figures. What did you tell them?"

"Just that they were wrong. I set up a story for you, like you told me. I told 'em—"

"Never mind, never mind. They got me identified for sure?"

"I don't know, Chuck. Maybe not. But enough to dig up the works if you come back."

Charley kept still after that because it was worse than ever. Don't come back, hide someplace else, maybe let me know where you are in a while and I send you your suitcase. Or maybe you don't even need your stuff seeing the way you're going to be traveling, seeing you're going to be needing a total change anyway.

"That's how it is, Chuck. Anything you want?"

And then again this would be the time for everybody to do a little pushing, except Charley of course. He'd be the one that gets the push. Chuck pushing out, the *cara-*

binièri pushing after, Uncle Sam pushing up with some
unfinished business—

"—and better don't call any more," said Joe, and
Charley could just see that mouth hanging open, the eyes
looking lazy and maybe Fanny was standing there, within
reach unless there was a new model by then.

"I won't," said Charley.

It didn't sound like the same voice to Joe. Something
had happened at the other end of the line, something that
he better know about. Then Charley told him.

"I'm coming back. With bells on."

He hung up, went back to the bar. He wasn't limping
any more. While he paid his bill he looked around the
room like he knew what he wanted.

"And gimme an empty glass," he said to the barman
who brought the change.

"And keep the change," he said when he got the glass.
Then he went and sat down where Delmont was, holding
the bottle.

The drunk had been coasting with just a nip here and
there because what he mostly wanted was talk. That tourist bastard was okay. A little out of focus maybe and kind
of snotty when he opened his mouth but he didn't talk
much. He listened. He didn't impress much but that
would come, tourist bastards always impressed after a
while. Might even be good for some fun, or a sucker play.
Somebody was due for a sucker play right around then
because Delmont himself had been getting it in the neck
lately, too much lately, like getting the boot from that
buddy bastard Amir in Cairo, like being stranded with
just one bottle left between him and the screaming wil-
lies—so when Charley sat down and took the bottle out
of his hand it was a surprise. Charley poured into his glass,
gave the bottle back, and hoisted his glass.

"To Delmont," he said and drank.

If Delmont had known that Charley never drank, almost never, he would have watched out. He would have
held on to his bottle and made a beeline for the first open
door or window or crack in the wall.

"Hey," he said and worked his tongue around that tooth.

"That's better, Delmont. Talk it up. Make it gay. Come
on, up on your feet. This place is too noisy. I can hardly
hear what you're saying."

"Hey," said Delmont, but Charley had him up and talked friendly.

"Where's your room, buddy? You got a room?"

"What in hell—"

"So you can talk some more. Big shot like you ought to have lots to talk about. All right, big shot. You do the talking and I bring the bottle. A full one, big shot."

"Upstairs," said Delmont. "Upstairs in the back. And you bring the—"

"Yeah. I'll bring the.".

Charley got a quart of bar cognac and steered the drunk to the rear. There were doors all along the corridor and in back, where the lightbulb hung, there was a staircase. The downstairs rooms didn't have permanent guests, just rabbit jobs like the two sailors. But upstairs you could stay all night, even longer. Maybe it wouldn't take all night, Charley was thinking. Plan it right, get to work with no small talk in between, and maybe it wouldn't take all night. It wouldn't take a month, that was a cinch. After all, what's four questions?

Delmont opened the room in back and switched on the light. There was a bed, a table, two chairs, and a suitcase under the bed. The drunk looked around, then at Charley, as if he was waiting to be commended. In the adjoining room somebody giggled.

"This one's on me," said Charley and plunked the full bottle on the table.

Delmont got it open and drank. There was a small window behind the drunk. It gave out to a blind wall where a storehouse backed up to the yard. Charley watched the wall and waited for Delmont to get done with the bottle.

When Delmont was through he wheezed in his throat, put the bottle down and eyed Charley. Charley was smiling again. Cold-nosed like a dog. One queer sucker, thought Delmont. Better have one more drink. But now Charley had the bottle, filling his glass, and then he hoisted it like before.

"To Delmont," he said.

Chapter Six

"Number one," said Charley. "Tell me about that Amir."

"To hell with that Amir. Him and me is through. Are through," he added.

"Fine. When will you see him again?"

"Never!" yelled Delmont. "That pig darsen't show his face over here, and good riddance."

"You saw to that, eh, big shot?"

The drunk liked that so he laid it on thick. "For once, buddy boy, I didn't have to lift a finger. Amir can't get in the country anyway. They don't think he's desirable. So I didn't have to do a thing."

"Fine friends you got, big shot."

"Friends! I'll kill that bastard next time I see him! Five years in Cairo I show that bastard the ropes, introduce him to all the right elements, and then, so help me—"

"I know. He dumped you."

"Wanna know what that bastard is doing? He—"

"Never mind, big shot."

"He sells dope. I show him how. I show him the ropes and then he don't trust me—me, his buddy—and gives me the boot."

"Nice guy, big shot. He coulda just set you up for a hit. Save himself a trip back to Italy."

The drunk got sly then and looked around like in a melodrama. "Not to me he wouldn't do that, tourist buddy. I got powerful friends!"

"And they wouldn't want you any deader."

"That's right, buddy, and Amir knows it. All the time I kept telling Amir don't bend a hair on my head, Amir buddy, I got powerful friends here—"

"Okay, that's enough."

Charley pushed the bottle over, which interrupted the drunk. Number one was fine. Question number one was out of the way. Delmont had been in Cairo, maybe five years, and he wasn't likely to run into that crowd over here. And when he came back he didn't go through Customs.

"Number two," said Charley.

"Two what, buddy boy?"

"Who's Bantam?"

The drunk looked at the wall between here and the next room. There was mumbling and the sound of a bed.

"Rabbits," said the drunk.

"Who's Bantam?"

The drunk made a disgusted face. "Like I was telling you, buddy boy, he's my powerful friend. He's in business here, and what he says goes. He says no to Amir and Amir don't operate. That's who Bantam is, and he's a buddy of mine."

That's who Bantam was, only the drunk had it backwards. Bantam was from the States and all he was doing was keeping up the contacts. He got paid from the States, he did what his bosses told him to do, and he was middle man for some of the syndicate's business that went through Italy and maybe the Near East. If Amir was anything to Bantam, he was one of his suppliers. In that circle Bantam was small potatoes. To Charley he wasn't. To Charley he was a man who knew Delmont.

"He'd give you his right arm, eh, big shot?"

"Sure. Haven't seen old Bantam in maybe ten years, but we're buddies. Always been."

"Sure. You set him up in business."

"That's right, tourist buddy, that's how it was. One day I meet Bantam—in Milano, I think—and being a countryman I take him in hand. He just got here. Green, I tell you, real green."

"So you set him up."

"Fixed him up. I show him this house where they got nothing but the best. High class from all over the world. You don't just walk in there, buddy boy, and say 'how about a jump?' You gotta be introduced!"

"You introduce him."

"Yeah. I show him the house. We been buddies ever since."

"You get your cut, buddy?"

"Cut? This was friendship, you bastard. Like the other time. The other time—in Genoa, I think—I see him in that café there just by chance. I walk up to Bantam and say, 'How'd you like some more of the same? Right here in Genoa?" I don't wait for an answer but run right over where I know this chick—I mean nice all around—and take her back to the café."

"And Bantam is so horny since Milano he takes her right around the corner."

"He wasn't there," said the drunk. "Been called away on business. That's how big my buddy is. Sitting right there in that café—"

"That's enough, big shot," and Charley pushed the bottle over.

So number two was out of the way. Delmont didn't know Bantam from Adam.

"Number three," he said. This time he had to take the bottle away because Delmont had started to feel low. Delmont let go of the bottle but he almost fell off the chair, that's how little he cared.

"And me that showed him the ropes, me—" Then he noticed the bottle was gone and turned mean again. "Look, tourist, get one thing. Nobody messes with Delmont, hear? Gimme that bottle, tourist."

When Charley wasn't fast enough the drunk spat in his face, from right across the table.

"You hear, tourist?"

Charley just wiped his face.

"I'm going downstairs now, tourist, and get that girl. Time those rabbits were off and gone, and when I come back you better be gone. I hate Peeping Toms, tourist."

"I'm not, big shot. I'm not even making a peep. Here's your bottle."

"You wanna stay, huh? Wanna see how she screams, huh? I learned ways in Cairo, buddy boy, and I give no quarter!" He had started declaiming. "They mess with Delmont and they don't even get a nickel!"

"Sit down, Casanova."

"What did you call me?"

"Big shot."

"Gimme that bottle."

"Number three," said Charley and he drank from his glass. His head was starting to pound, but that was better than the feel of pressure inside his chest, a pressure like any minute something was going to explode. Just a little while longer and then there would be no more of that ache, as if he were running without a breath but running to catch one.

"You got big friends," said Charley. "You got any little ones? Just common-type people, like downstairs, like in Rome, in Naples—"

"Bastards," said the drunk.

"Or Genoa?"

"Never been in Naples. Not since the place on Ischia."

"In Thirty-five."

"Before."

"Don't get around much any more, huh, big shot?"

"I get around. I get around plenty!"

"And make lots of buddies all over."

"I don't got the time, buddy boy. I don't bother with small fry. Only reason I bring you up here is because you asked me. And I don't often do favors, buddy boy, so watch your step."

"That's why you haven't got any friends, big shot. You're too big."

"I got lots of 'em, boy. Don't you worry."

"But I do," said Charley, and he smiled.

"Well, don't. I don't. Good riddance to those bastard friends."

"What happened?"

"I run outa dough, that's what happened, you bastard friend!"

"I know how it is, big shot. They sponge on you while you're good for it and—"

"Naw. My friends is loaded. They don't sponge."

Charley waited.

"Know how I lost my dough, buddy?"

"At the tables."

"The tables! You couldn't lose that much dough at the tables! In the Crash, boy, in the big Crash!"

That was a long time ago. So must have been Delmont's friends. He lost his dough in the Crash, sold his place on Ischia, stuck around, drifted, ended up the way he was now. Maybe he still had an income, some rich aunt back in the States. . .

"Made it all myself, boy. Every cent! I was made for that market, boy. When I hit New York from down New Hampshire way, I started running circles around that market. I—"

"That's enough," said Charley, but this time he let the man have the bottle. He hadn't had any friends since '29.

"And now number four," said Charley and then he

waited a minute because his head was going like mad. There was a head inside a head and they went in opposite directions.

"You don't look healthy," said the drunk. "Maybe you think I stink or something."

"Yeah."

"Maybe you're laughing up your sleeve and calling me a liar, you sonofabitch."

Charley hardly caught the tone of his voice so he just said, "Yeah," and held his head.

When the drunk was all over him with vicious kicks and nails clawing it would have been easy to make him stop. But the drunk might pass out. He might go cold and never answer number four. Charley pushed him off like he was saving the guy. Then the drunk stopped. He was panting in the middle of the room, wanting to fight— better yet, wanting to do some big damage.

"What did you call me, buddy?"

"I called you a liar."

"You? Calling me?"

"That's right," said Charley and he tried to think hard how to get to the point. "Because you can't prove a thing," he said finally. "All night you're gassing at me, about Egypt and Amir, about landing here without passport, about being Italian and U.S.A. all at the same time—"

Charley waited. One thing about drunks, they always haul out the billfold and prove everything with papers. They haul out a library card to prove they can read. They haul out a baby picture to show they can make babies. And when really pressed they come up with their Mason's card where it says Smith or something to prove they are Smith or something.

"Okay," said Delmont, and he felt he had landed a sucker.

He got the suitcase and opened it. He looked at Charley over his shoulder. "Stand back, buddy. You're peeping."

When he turned back to the suitcase and pulled out underwear, someone in the next room gave a low laugh.

"What you say, tourist?" And the drunk spun around.

But Charley just stood there looking blank. His hands had started to tremble but he kept his face blank. And then the laugh again, from the next room.

"Out of my way!" the drunk said, and charged to the door. Charley saw how he threw it open and heard the crack when he tore into the next room. Then Charley didn't listen any more. He turned to the suitcase.

First there was more underwear. There was a revolver in one of the socks and there was an unfinished letter.

And an Italian passport.

It was dog-eared and ancient. It had expired in 1938 and the picture in it was Delmont all right, looking meaner because there was muscle in his face and looking flashy as a matinee idol, with mustache, hair on the head, and a flower in the pinstriped suit. Delmont had changed from bastard to bum.

There was a sheet folded along old and worn creases and it said: Monarchy of Italy . . . hereby grants . . . to Richard Delmont, Citizenship of the Sovereign State of Italy. And some other details.

There was an old ration card, dated 1944.

There was a driver's license.

A war registration, showing Delmont unfit.

Then the scream.

It brought Charley back, and all the noise from next door made awesome sense. "I got my buddy next door!" Delmont was screaming, "and once I call the cops we give testimony! I bet when your wife hears . . . "

Charley moved fast. The drunk would scream enough to stir up the whole house, and the larger the audience the sooner the *carabinièri.*

The girl was on the bed holding a sheet in front of her and the man stood there naked and didn't care how it looked. He took a short step toward Delmont and talked low. Just the voice alone should have scared Delmont.

"The *carabinièri!*" yelled the drunk. "You aren't married, you raping bastard, and the kid's no more than twelve if she's a day!"

Before Charley was halfway into the room Delmont reached for the sheet and tore it away from the girl.

There wasn't a chance to get a good look at her. The man jumped at Delmont like a snake striking prey. Let the bastard get killed, Charley thought. He was out in the corridor again when he froze. Maybe it was the gasp from the girl, or the wet sound out of Delmont's throat, but he turned and saw the man pull the knife out, and the drunk sank to the floor seeping blood.

He had to know. Charley came back and knelt next to Delmont, shaking him to find if he were still alive. The man had his pants on, and he slapped the girl's face to make her move. He got her up, threw a coat over her shoulders, and pushed her toward the door. He stopped with his shirt half on, grabbed the girl's arm with one hand and with the other one pointed the knife toward Charley. He held it steady.

"It was you," said the man. "Look at him, Rosa." He shook the girl. "It was this one!"

"It was this one," she said, and the man tossed the knife across the drunk's belly. It landed right next to his hand but he couldn't use it. The drunk was dead.

Chapter Seven

To Charley it couldn't have been more complete, the way it had solved itself and he had won. When he stuffed the papers into his pocket, Charley Delmont—for one moment at least—felt free. But then his head started again with a slow throb, and the ache in his side wanted to double him over. It wasn't the worst, though. The worst came when he left the drunk's room and passed the door where the body was.

He and the drunk had been sitting downstairs, and Charley had bought a bottle of cognac at the bar, and then he and the drunk had gone up to the room.

After they found the body they would find the man and his girl—and then they would find Charley. "It was you!" the man would say, and the girl, "It was this one!"

There was no other way.

He went into the room, closed the drying knife, put it into his pocket. When he turned the body there was very little blood because the knife had been thin. He carried the drunk from this room to the next, closed the door, and opened the window. He threw out the body. When it hit, Charley was ready, holding his breath and his hands on the window frame like clamps. But there was hardly a sound, just a soft thud. He kept waiting for more.

He closed the window and went to the bed. He put everything back into the suitcase except the gun, and then closed the suitcase. He put the gun in his pocket and went downstairs. It should have felt easy the way it worked. Nobody saw him going downstairs, the back door was dark, and so was the yard. Charley picked up the body, heaved it over the fence next to the warehouse, and climbed over himself. He left the body where it was, walked down the alley, and a few streets later he found his Bugatti.

He backed into the alley and curled the body inside the big trunk. First he drove west, toward the coast where the tide might take the thing out; but when the buildings thinned and he hit the stretch of road that took him out to the open, he stopped. He stopped, turned around, and

38

went the other way. He didn't much think about it, but
it was safer where the dark houses crowded in, where
nobody would think of taking a Sunday walk, where the
slow Tiber wormed her way under the old bridges and
the smell in the air was bad. That's where the dead drunk
belonged; that's where Charley Delmont would feel better
about it.

But he made a mistake and hit the Via Veneto, where
the sidewalk cafés and the big hotels made a ballroom
light all along the street. He got caught in the late evening traffic and for a few blocks he had to crawl down the
boulevard with every expensive car in Europe jamming
him in. Charley Delmont didn't look out of place. He
looked tanned, as if he had nothing to do but lie in the
sun all day, and his Bugatti was a low, big-wheeled racer.
Charley Delmont looked as if he belonged.

He had to stop at a crossing to let the party-goers get
by. They wore evening clothes, the men in white jackets
and the women in bare, glittering things, and laughing.
They patted the long hood of his car and told him how
nice it looked. He tried to smile back at them but it
didn't work. He felt sick in the head with an off-center
spinning that seemed to twist his face to one side. Then he
let the car crawl again. He thought he would feel better
once the dark streets started again, but it got worse. The
slow creeping got worse all the time, wouldn't get better
till he got rid of the dead load in the trunk. He could hear
it every so often, when the ruts got bad.

He had swung off the Via Veneto, heading back to the
Tiber and across a bridge into Trastevere. The section was
dark with small, winding streets, with old houses along the
river and broken banks. When the ruts got worse the
thump in the trunk sounded like *ridofit, ridofit, ridofit.*
It got worse going downhill, worse going uphill, until
Charley kept gunning the motor to make a new sound.

Think of it in a different way; think of the black history
along the river, the intrigue, the loves and the fortunes
that changed hands every time a dead man fell into the
river. Where did the Sforzas throw their enemies off the
bridges, or the Borgias throw their friends off the bridges?
When they were around there was great gusto to the whole
thing and they didn't care who heard the splash. Or Nero,
the daddy of them all—he did it alive. Real strong stuff,
with gusto.

When he stopped the car it was nothing like that at all. Nobody was watching, nobody was letting out a cheer because now he'd be rid of it, and the black air was dead with the stillness in it. Charley opened the trunk. He knew the body was in there. He couldn't see it but there it was, reeking of whisky as if the drunk were still breathing. Charley held on to the lid a minute to make things steady. There wasn't a sound, but inside his head it spun around with a whir like *ridofit, ridofit.*

He carried the dead drunk maybe two blocks, where the canal was on one side of the street and blind-looking houses along the other. Then the bridge. A fine old bridge with the silhouette of a giant tiara.

Charley climbed down to the water, under the arch. It was dank, like a high-roofed cave, down there, as if there ought to be a cold wind coming through. There wasn't. It was warm and moist and no wind. Where the leg of the bridge went down into the water it was bound to be deep. There was no current and once the dead drunk came up again it wouldn't matter any more.

Charley let him down near the water, put stones in his pockets. Maybe some iron would help. He didn't have to stay down there long, but a piece of iron would help. The tow chain from the car. A two-block walk. He couldn't do it, not if he had to come back. The railing along the canal, up by the street where the old railing had fallen over. Charley went up the bank again and worked one of the posts off the crossbars. A nice, heavy post with a cast flower on top. A lily, maybe. He shoved it under the body's belt, buttoned the shirt and jacket around it so the thing was along the chest, just like a lily.

Get rid of it.

There wasn't even a splash, just bubble sounds. He dropped the knife after it and when the bubble sounds stopped, Charley was rid of it.

He came out from under the arch reaching for air, and when he had taken a breath he leaned against the leg of the bridge and exhaled. It came out as a moan but he didn't care. He was rid of it. He took another deep breath, head back, so that's when he saw her.

She was leaning over the side of the bridge, just a shape, and the way her hair hung down around her face it made the head look very large.

To Charley she looked like a monster.

Chapter Eight

SHE DIDN'T MOVE, and he couldn't until he saw her lean out further and raise an arm.

"Hello! You!"

He didn't catch the question in her voice, only the fact that it was human. Then he acted by instinct, yanked out the gun, and aimed up.

"You down there—" he heard again but not the rest. As he turned the pain in his side boiled over, twisted the girl on the bridge out of focus. For a moment he felt as if he had to throw up and he became so weak he could barely balance himself. He gasped, rested, holding on to the bank.

When his strength came back it came slowly, with the first rush gone out of it. It came from the brain so that he knew what he had to do—only he didn't do it. He tried, he broke out in a sweat. He tried but the gun wouldn't come up. If he could stop everything now—but if he stopped now it would mean he had to run forever.

The rage crawled through him like a flush, slow and hot, and he started up the embankment. He turned to the bridge with the gun in his hand, probing it ahead of him.

She stood motionless in the half-light and again the hair around her head made it look like before, very large. As long as she didn't move it was like a spell on him, and he started to kill her every step of the way. He didn't rush her, he stalked. Every step of the way—until she moved.

"Are you all right?" she asked.

His strength, which was nothing but hate, struck a wall.

"If you are sick—" she started, and he felt how his lips tasted like paper and a muscle jerked in his back. There was a painful rust in his joints. He stopped. He leaned against the stone railing and waited. Perhaps she would run. If she would only run. If only something would happen, something fast and sudden.

"Rest a moment," she said. "Then I'll help you across

41

the bridge—" and she came toward him with the half-light making it all very slow and soft— "across the bridge," she said. "I live very close."

He could see her face now and he saw that only her hair was big. Her face was small, but for the moment he couldn't tell if it was small like a child's or small because she was delicate. An attractive face. The thought woke him and he shook his head. Now if she were a monster— What next, her beautiful breasts, her beautiful belly, her crazy beautiful legs. Next perhaps? How many lire? Crazy out of his head—

"Take my arm," she said. "You don't look too well. We go across—"

"Wait a minute. Wait a minute."

Crazy beautiful legs, he thought. How did he know? He couldn't tell how she looked. She was dressed dark, a knit jacket; only her face showed in the dark.

"Wait a minute," he said again because he had to hear the sound of his voice once more to slow down his head. It helped. It helped him remember she had leaned over the bridge because she had heard something, she had stood there when he thought he had been alone. Only one thing to do—only one thing—

"Later," she said. "You can rest better later. The night air here isn't—"

Later was good. Not as good, but meanwhile stick close, don't let her get away. Hold on. Charley Delmont holding on so he wouldn't have to run—

"I'll hold on," he said and took her arm. His fingers went around her arm with a slow pressure, not getting too hard, just holding there.

They walked.

Now that he had decided, it wasn't so difficult any more. First, stick close. Then, her place.

"Do you live with your parents?"

"No. I have a room."

Get her out of Rome some way, get her to talk. What did you see, what was I doing, what do you want— If she didn't answer it right, that was that. If she wouldn't answer at all—worse.

"My arm," she said. "You are—"

He relaxed a little.

She took him through the house that faced the street and across the court, then into the narrow building in

back. It smelled old inside. Down the hall she opened a
door. They went through the door and he leaned against
it while she lit a lamp.

"Sit on the bed," she said.

"I'm all right."

When the light was on she saw him clearly for the
first time. She had thought he looked softer, but now his
cheekbones looked sharp, his eyes looked at her without
blinking, and the smile on his mouth wasn't right. But
he still leaned, like in pain. When he kept looking at her
she suddenly felt uneasy.

"You got aspirin?" he asked.

She didn't answer but started to look in a drawer. The
bureau was old and it was hard to open the drawer because of the bed. There was just the bureau, the bed,
and a chair. She knew there were no aspirin, but she
looked for a while longer before she turned. She didn't
like to feel frightened.

"I don't have aspirin," she said. "I can ask upstairs."

He didn't move from the door. "Don't go. Just let me
stand a minute."

She watched him. "Are you ill?"

Better say yes. "It comes and goes," he said.

"Perhaps you need a doctor. I can run to the Via Ales-
sandria and bring him."

Still wanted to get away. He didn't look sick enough.
The weakness from before was going away—he tried to
forget it—and maybe he wouldn't wait any longer. But
not yet, not here. It was still too soon after the bridge— He
took a breath and made it sound painful.

"I got aspirin, in the car. Walk me to the other side
of the bridge, to my car."

She didn't hesitate, because that was how she had
started, trying to help him, and they walked back across
the bridge, to the alley where he had parked the car.
She stood by while he leaned over the door and went
through the glove compartment. But of course there was
nothing. Then he climbed behind the wheel. It made him
wince, which was good, because she ran up and said,
"Are you all right? Where is your aspirin?"

He rested behind the wheel to make sure she'd feel
safe.

"No aspirin. Look—" He waited a moment. "Look, I
gotta buy some," and didn't have to say any more.

"I will go with you, but I do not drive. You must drive carefully and I help you watch."

Then she climbed into the seat next to him and Charley started the car. They didn't look at each other. She watched the road and sometimes she looked at the car, the chrome fittings and the leather.

"Are you an American?"

"My name's Charley."

"I am Martha."

He hadn't paid much attention before, but now he noticed her more. He noticed her voice, which sounded warm even though she talked fast. He wondered about her again, about what she had seen at the bridge, why she came along—

"What were you doing under the bridge?" she asked. "Had you fallen?"

"I fell. I got weak and rolled down."

"But the guard rail—"

"It's broken."

"You're right. It's been broken for a long time."

"How long?"

"Since I've been here. Before, probably."

"Tell me, Martha—"

"I know. I came to Rome to get married, but he had left."

So she wasn't too young.

"Why don't you go back, wherever that is?"

She shrugged as if it didn't matter, but then she laughed, not pleasantly.

"He left me without marrying," she said.

Perhaps the guy had good reason. Charley couldn't tell. Perhaps he should have left her on the bridge, in the Tiber maybe. She had already told him more than most women would, but he only knew less about her. It sounded simple, almost as simple as if he had asked her "how many lire" and she had told him.

"How many lire?" he said.

"What?"

"Nothing."

She turned to him and when he looked at her face he saw that she had understood. He could not imagine what she would do next.

"You said how many lire."

"My mistake."

"You are right. And you said it because you are sick, perhaps."

"That's right, Martha."

She turned front but wasn't through.

"You lie again," she said.

Charley turned the car through a square. "What else did I lie about, kid?"

"My name is Martha," she said and wouldn't talk more.

He felt nettled. He thought it was good to feel this way because that way it would be easier later. "What else did I lie about, Martha?"

"You think I'm a prostitute."

"Does it insult you?"

"No. Because you are wrong. And I try to remember that you are sick. A fever maybe."

He didn't think she was a whore. She had tried nothing. She hadn't even opened her ragged wool jacket which she kept buttoned over her dress. But he didn't think she had led a very sheltered life since coming to Rome. Or maybe she had. There was nothing weak about her, the way she had decided to help him, the way she had thrown his insult back in his face.

"Turn here," she said. "When you come to the boulevard go two blocks. The apothecary there is open all night. I will get your pills, and then you go. I go home alone."

He swung out of the narrow street and took the boulevard. It had lights in the middle, and dark office buildings on either side. The lighted apothecary was ahead, at the corner where a streetcar crossed the boulevard, and all Charley had to do was make a U-turn, head back into the maze of dark streets, and get his business done. He still knew nothing about her watching him from that bridge. She may well be the kind who would never say anything, no matter what she had seen. It would not be anything new to him. He had relied on it himself often enough, that a peasant wouldn't talk who had seen him unload stolen goods in the hills somewhere; or the time when he jumped the *carabinière*, slugged him unconscious, and the old woman who had seen it from the balcony had turned her head and just kept stroking her cat.

But then he didn't have to decide. Before he had time to think more he suddenly jammed on the brake and stopped. Martha flew forward, but Charley didn't. His head was already down on the steering wheel and his color was green.

"Charley," she started, "what has—"

"Wait." She could barely hear him.

"Charley!"

"Wait," he said again. His hand crept over, held her arm like a vise.

He needn't have held her. She sat still watching him breathe and then how the color came back to his face.

"Martha. Here in my pocket. Money."

"My arm," she said.

He let go and she reached into his jacket. That's when she felt the blood where his wound had opened.

"Get the money," he said.

"You are badly—"

"I know. Buy bandages, big ones. Get iodine, adhesive, and a bottle of aspirin. And a small box."

"What, Charley?"

"Small box of aspirin. I like to carry a small box of—" he kept his head down on the wheel and waved her off.

It was better when she came back. He could sit up without feeling dizzy and the pain was just dull. Martha was running.

"Here," she said. "Open your shirt."

"Never mind. Sit still."

He took the aspirin box and put it in his pocket. Then he opened the bottle and shook pills into his hand. He put them under his tongue.

"And take this," she said. There was a short tube in her hand and when she broke it she held it to his face. The strong odor stung up his nose.

"Hold still," she said. He had to inhale it.

"Now open your shirt."

He pushed her hand away, started the car.

"You can come to my room," she said. "Drive slowly and it may stop bleeding."

He drove off, in the wrong direction.

"Martha, listen. I've been shot. I can't stay here. In Rome, in the outskirts, maybe, just out of town—"

"Drive carefully, Charley," she said, so there was nothing more to discuss. He headed for the inland highway to Naples and just out of town he turned off. He kept sniffing the aromatic she had brought along because it

cleared his eyes, kept his brain from reeling off. But the
alertness was only behind his eyes or on the top of his
head. His body felt like in a shroud, with vague movements that never quite made it.

When he thought of the girl, Martha, he felt himself
get confused, even though she had made it all so simple.
She had said, I'll come along if you want help; she had
told him how she came to be alone, and that she wasn't
selling a thing. Somehow she had also told him that she
was not afraid, because she probably didn't have anything
that was precious.

She had not told him what she had seen from the
bridge.

"Stop here, Charley. You are passing the *pensione*."

He hadn't even seen it. He noticed later how she arranged for the room, for hot water, and how she kept the
proprietor from asking questions. In the room she undressed him and cleaned the wound. She made it hurt with
the iodine but paid no attention when he started to curse.
She bandaged him and then went downstairs. He didn't
stop her. She came back with a glass of milk and he
drank it.

There was only one bed. He lay under the blanket
watching her unbutton the jacket. Then she took off her
dress. She looked light brown in the light from the oil
lamp, and very firm. Her breasts made round shadows.
She walked across the room as if he weren't there. She
lay down next to him, doing it carefully.

"No," she said. "Go to sleep."

He did. He just remembered that she was soft to the
touch. Then he slept.

Chapter Nine

AFTER TWO DAYS Charley felt better. She could tell by the way he watched her when she got out of the bed in the morning. She dressed quickly and when she looked shapeless again she sat down on the bed.

"You feel better, Charley."

"Worse. Three nights in bed like this can kill a man."

She laughed and folded her arms. "It gave you your strength back."

"It's started to make my ears pop. Come here," and he reached for her.

She got up, out of the way, and the mood changed. He got out of bed and dressed.

"Three nights," he said, "and I don't know you at all." He left his shirt off and went to the washstand. The air felt cold in the room. "Martha," he said and smiled. "How many lire, Martha?"

She didn't smile back. She watched him wash and said, "Three nights and you still don't know."

He flipped some water at her but it didn't help the mood. She wiped her cheek and looked past him.

"How many lire, Martha?"

She shrugged.

"What's it take, Martha. Love?"

"When you excite me. That is a good start."

He stopped trying to joke with her and shaved.

After breakfast in the dark *ristorante* downstairs he told her he was going to Rome. He didn't have to tell her to come because he knew she was going back. He wasn't sick any more, so she was leaving. He hadn't excited her, so she was leaving.

They stepped out into the sun that glared back at them from the white houses. Only the shadows were black, and the cypresses on the dry hills. And Martha's hair. He realized he had never seen her by sunlight, her small face, the eyes that seemed to turn blacker in the light, and how she walked like the women who carry baskets on their heads. Only her clothes looked shabby. In the light they had no color at all.

48

They got into the car. They still hadn't said anything else. He put two aspirins under his tongue and drove.

"Are you in pain?" she asked.

"No."

"Because of those pills. You always eat those pills."

"Just a habit," he said. "Like smoking. You smoke, Martha?"

"Sometimes."

"What else do you do, Martha? Besides standing on bridges and so forth?"

"I work in a bakery."

"What else?"

"The way you smile always I don't know if you are just talking or whether you want to know."

"Just a habit."

"I think so. Your smile and your aspirin, they are both like habits."

At the Rome highway he turned right. Maybe half an hour to Rome. After two days and three nights, half an hour was left to find out what he had to know. As soon as he would stop in Rome she would get out of the car and leave. Half an hour to decide what to do with her. When he thought about it and remembered what he had started to do—to kill her—his smile was suddenly gone. If she were still the monster on the bridge, it might be easy. So why hadn't he done it then, before she turned into a woman, before she had gone with him as if it was the natural thing to do. Three nights in bed with her and nothing. Natural!

"Martha."

"Yes?"

"We'll be in Rome soon. Maybe half an hour."

"I know."

"When we get there—I want to buy you some clothes."

She looked at him. Her eyebrows were up and half her mouth was smiling.

"How many lire, Charley?" But this time he didn't think it was funny and when she saw it she stopped smiling and said, "Why, Charley?"

He knew why, and the reason was very simple. None of the complicated reasons were behind it.

"Because I want you to look good."

This time she really smiled. She looked at her knit

jacket with the drooping pockets at the side. She had ugly shoes on, very heavy, and she rubbed them together.

"What else, Charley?"

"You know. Might get you excited."

She looked at him but not at the face. She looked where his bandage was under the shirt.

"Those three nights," she said. "I knew they would bother you."

"You're damn right," he said.

She moved so her knee touched his but then she took it away again. It had happened by chance.

"Charley," she said, "it does not excite me to get clothes from you."

"You'd be a queer duck if that's all it took."

"But I would like to have them."

"Sure."

"I like to look good to you."

"That's no problem."

"In clothes, too."

"That'll be no problem. If I pick 'em."

They were going faster, and Martha held the handle on the dashboard in front of her. She held it with one hand and it made her turn half his way.

"I too thought they were three strange nights."

"Strange. I didn't mean strange, kid."

"I did. You didn't excite me then."

She held the handle in one hand and stroked the leather of the seat with the other. The leather had a smell like hot skin. It felt hot under her hand.

"What about your job? The bakery?"

"I can get another."

"After staying away a week?"

"It's only been two days."

"Plus another three nights makes almost a week."

"One night, Charley. I don't know yet about afterwards."

"You gotta give me more odds, kid. After all, I'm not a well man.

"Who knows how you will be after one night?" she said and they laughed about it.

In the outskirts of Rome traffic slowed them down. Charley drove and Martha sat back in her seat. There was nothing to say, so he had to start thinking of the other thing again, the unsettled business. Joe Lenken would have done it the other way around. First the business, then the excitement. But Joe was such a hot planner none of this would have happened to him in the first place. And if it had and he stuck to business first—what would be left after?

The thought felt ugly and he couldn't look at Martha next to him on the seat. He chewed his lip, got the little box out of his pocket. He put the two pills under his tongue automatically. He stopped for a light, started again with the gears meshing wrong. She probably hadn't seen a thing; too dark on that bridge. If she had she wouldn't have acted like she did for two days. She would have given herself away. Or perhaps not, what did he know of her?

Enough, he figured. She'd just shown him. Tramp off with a stranger, to hell with the job, and if he buys her some duds let him roll her in bed for a night. He figured that was the neat way to look at it and that's how he'd keep her around. Till he got her straight—and if she was straight maybe keep her a while longer.

Charley stopped a few houses away from Alivar's bookstore. He pulled some lire notes out of his pocket, folded them, put them in Martha's hand.

"Remember the store we passed two blocks down? Buy yourself something. From the skin out."

"And you?" She was putting the notes into her pocket without having counted them.

"When you're through, meet me up ahead, in the bookstore. Where it says Alivar. How long will you be?"

"An hour? But I also want to go back to my room. I have—"

"Forget it. Whatever you need, buy it and come back here. Okay?"

She nodded and said she would. He watched her walk off, wondering how she would look when she came back. He was that sure of her.

The business with Alivar didn't take long. Alivar recognized him immediately. Charley browsed along the stalls and toward the rear. Then he browsed right along through a curtain and into a small room in back. Alivar was there and Charley showed him the papers. They talked about what was to be changed, how long it would take, and the job would be five hundred thousand lire.

Charley paid half in advance and said he'd be back next evening. Then he browsed some more.

When the neat-looking girl walked toward him he had to give her a double take before he was sure. Martha was something. Black hair blacker against the white shirt, and the shirt making a fine thrust in front, tucked into a belt that held her waist so the hips flared out. The skirt was straight and lighter than the tone of her legs. The whole thing looked simple and ended up making her twice as feminine. Either she had an instinct for it or somebody who knew about clothes had done the job for her.

"Christ," he said.

She just turned and patted herself.

"Let's go," he said, and she walked out of the store ahead of him.

There were more boxes in the car so he put them into the trunk. Then they took off. But before he left Rome he swung up the Via Veneto again where the sidewalk cafés made a confusion along both sides. He parked and took her to a café with boxhedges around the tables, and they sat under the frosted glass roof which slanted over the sidewalk. She had never been in a place like this. He knew that because she had told him so but she sat down, not feeling wrong about it, and ordered *Monte Bianco*.

"I love sweets," she said. "In the bakery I always eat sweets when nobody is looking." Then she started spooning and didn't talk for a while.

He wondered how she stayed so trim eating Italian sweets all the time. He wondered how anybody could eat more than maybe a spoonful of *Monte Bianco*. He sucked his aspirin and drank black coffee.

They left Rome, going south. He took the coastal highway this time and he listened to her describe the view. She talked about it as if she thought he were blind. He hadn't said much and when he passed the sign that said Nettuno and Anzio, giving less than ten kilometers, he took the first crossroad inland and didn't talk any more at all. Martha stopped talking too.

He could have stopped several times, when they passed a town, or just by the road where shady growths climbed along hillsides. He started to go faster, mostly uphill, snapping around turns and gunning the motor when the road made a short dip. The sun was back of them now and Martha held the thick hair away from her neck. Charley

started to feel the way his car sounded; the on-and-off
racing of the big engine straining uphill, getting just so
high and stopping because the pull was over. And then
another small hill, one after the other, but never high
enough to give the engine a full roar.

"Charley," she said, "where are you going?"

He kept looking ahead.

"You know where I'm going."

"Yes, I know. When, Charley?"

"What's the matter, can't wait?"

She flinched but he didn't see it. He thought there was
nothing that he could do to really offend her. That's
how he wanted to feel about her.

"Answer me."

She reached into the leather bag she had bought and
pulled out a cigarette. Then she smoked.

"Would you like one?" she asked.

"You know I don't smoke."

"Yes, you told me. How is your pain?"

"I don't eat aspirin for pain. Just pleasure. And how's
yours?"

"What?"

"How do you feel, I said. How's it now? Still excited?"

"It is very exciting the way you drive," she said. She
smoked with deep, even drags.

"Ya. I'm a hot driver, huh? You didn't think I was
such a hot driver. Or could be, when I came crawling out
from under that bridge."

"No," she said. "You looked bad."

"So would you, lying under moist bridges. Tell me,
Martha, how long did you see me lying there?"

"I don't know."

"But you saw me."

"I don't know if you were lying there. I heard a sound.
I saw something—"

"What sound?"

"You, Charley."

"Me. I got a million sounds. I can bark like a dog, fizz
like a highball, meow like a cat."

"Like a cat," she said. "I think you groaned then."

"Then when? What did you hear before?"

She wasn't sure what she had heard before and if he
had asked 'what did you see?' she wouldn't have known
what to say either. Because of the way he asked—because

of the way he wanted to be sure she had seen nothing.

She said, "Just the water under the bridge. It always makes some sound under the bridge."

"Sure, that's the way bridges are. Always making sounds under there. Dribble and splash and so forth."

She felt how he waited for her to say something, how he wanted to know what she knew. There had been no splash. There had been grunting and scuffling, and a moan, then soft water sounds—no. First the water sound and then moaning?

"You thinking about it?" he said and she had to hold very still not to show how right he had been. If he wouldn't try so hard to make her think about it she would never have given it another thought. It is better not to think about vague things because they may come out right or wrong, all depending upon your wishes. She had no wish to think about it, only he did. He must fear she had seen something wrong.

"Well?" he said and it was like a push.

It made her remember. He had walked along the other bank—it must have been Charley—walked with a stooping load. Or perhaps there had been two men walking—

"I saw nothing," she said suddenly.

"Oh? How come? You were right on top of me."

Then there had only been one man. Charley. There had been the water noise and his groan! Then he was staggering towards her—with a gun? And he was bleeding, but that she didn't know until later.

"I can't remember, Charley. The light—"

"You can't, or you won't?"

She turned on him as if she meant to strike.

"There was nothing! Even until my room I had hardly seen you, so how can I say—"

"All right, all right," he said, as if it didn't matter.

And it didn't matter to her. If she had hated him or he had been dangerous to her—on the bridge, in her room—perhaps she would have remembered clear, evil things about him because that's how the mind works. But it hadn't been like that; a sick man, running away, getting well. And he wanted her. She wanted to believe that he wanted her, for no reason but that.

"All you heard was me," he said, "making a meow like a cat."

She was glad he was through. "Yes. And the Tiber."

Now he knew that she wasn't sure what she had seen or heard—that she could be convinced either way. She was looking off to the right now, where red and yellow rocks lay the length of a slope. She didn't want to talk any more. She thought that his bad humor got worse with talking, and the way he drove, and the sun biting the back of his neck—if he would only stop soon.

He did. He stopped digging at her because the way she got quiet she might just hold it so much longer and turn on him. If she got hostile, who knows what she might remember or make up just to spite him. He didn't know if she was spiteful, but her voice getting too soft and talking more and more slowly was a new sign. Leave her alone. Stay with clothes and other things like that for a while.

He started heading north, toward Rome, to the village where they still had the room. The road got more even, so that after a while only the tires made a noise. Martha was leaning back, eyes closed, and he drove. He thought that the slight tension which hadn't left must be natural. Three nights in bed with her, and nothing.

It was still daylight outside when he closed the door of the room. He sat down and watched her undress. It took her longer this time. Once she looked at him and smiled, but the smile she saw on his face had been there before and she didn't know whether he had seen her.

They came together without looking at each other and at first she answered him. She wanted to. But his love-making became like an attack of hate so he never noticed when she stopped trying.

It was dark when he woke up. She wasn't in bed. First he saw the cigarette glow in the dark and then he saw her. She sat by the window looking out. She didn't know he was awake. Every so often she touched one breast with her hand. He must have hurt her, he thought.

"Martha?"

She turned her head.

"You all right?"

He saw her nod. "Yes, Charley."

He didn't remember if it had been lousy or whether he just felt lousy now. Perhaps she would tell him.

"Did you sleep?"

"No."

He felt himself getting angry so he kept still for a while.

"Come here and sleep."

"I'm not tired, Charley."

He took a deep breath and watched her smoke. If it had been that lousy she would have left. But she hadn't even dressed. Her silhouette was naked and he saw it in the short glow when she pulled on the cigarette. In the dark, with nobody to see, he didn't have the smile on his face, but she could hear him so he made it light.

"Waiting for me?" he said. "Waiting for me to come around?"

He saw her toss the stub out the window but she didn't say anything.

"Or cooling off in the night breeze, maybe?"

This time she got up, walked to the middle of the room. He couldn't tell her face, he only saw her put her hands on her hips, legs straight.

"Lemme ask you another one," he said because he didn't want her to say anything right then. "Why'd you stay?"

"I was smoking."

If he could see her face, if he knew her better—

"Why did you come?"

"How much were the clothes?" she said and for a minute he wasn't sure she had said it.

"Twenty-five thousand lire."

"Now you know why I stayed," she said. "And how many lire."

She kept standing there, a wide-legged shape in the middle of the room, waiting for him to cut back at her.

But he didn't. At first he didn't do anything and then, even though nobody could see it, his face relaxed. He got up, walked over to her, and his hand came around her waist.

"I did want you to have those clothes." He waited a moment. "But not now," he said.

She listened for more but that was all he had to say. Next day she didn't leave as she had decided.

Chapter Ten

THEY CAME IN by the coast road and because she wanted to see it, drove along the curve of the harbor. To the left Naples climbed up the hill; to the right lay the wide stretch of the bay. From where they stopped on the bank the water looked cluttered—the confused stalks of the fishing fleet, fat tugs, and further out some low tankers which moved so slowly they seemed not to be moving at all. Nothing looked clean except the white tourist ship by the dock. It lay still, like a display. Only the little flags down the guy wires made fast, crazy twinkles.

"Do you see the bay from where you live, Charley?"

"Yes. I'm high up."

"I think I will like it," she said.

He started the car, drove into the city. The sharp harbor smells disappeared and after a while there was just the hot smell of stone and asphalt. Then that too left. The car started climbing and they drove through the section called Pizzofalcone, where the houses seemed to push each other into narrow, leaning shapes.

"Like Trastevere," she said, "only it climbs and there is no river."

"We live higher up," he said. "There's more room."

"You live upstairs or down?" she wanted to know.

"They aren't tenements with courtyards. More like the country."

"And a garden?"

"It's a mess, though."

She thought that was fine too and then he got to the *osteria*, where he parked the Bugatti in the yard. They walked the rest of the way.

From the steps the view looked as if it hadn't moved since the last time he stood there. Then she stopped in the garden and said it certainly was a mess.

"Has its advantage," he said. "This is Joe's house. I told you about him. My house is back there, at the other end of the garden. Overgrown like this you can't see across."

They walked through the open kitchen door. Francesca was there, scrubbing the table.

"Joe in?" he said.

He had to repeat it in Italian and she said yes, he was
in the other room. They waited for Francesca to dry the
table, which smelled piney from the scrubbing. Then they
sat down.

"Get him," said Charley.

She shook her head.

"Why? He asleep?"

"No," she said. "He's in bed."

Martha didn't get it. Then Joe opened the door. He
looked big and lazy, and even when he saw Charley his
expression didn't change. He came in leaving the door
open because he didn't care. The girl sitting on the bed
in back was pulling a blouse down over her breasts. The
rest of her was still naked. Joe sat down at the table and
said, *"Buon giorno."*

"This is Joe," said Charley. "He's at stud this week.
And this is Martha. She's with me."

"Glad to meet you," said Joe and then he turned to
Charley. "Back for good?"

"Like I told you."

"I am thirsty," said Martha.

"He drinks only beer," said Charley. "Beer and milk.
You want—"

"There's *aranciata*," said Joe. "The women drink it."

"I like *aranciata*," said Martha, and Francesca brought
her a glass of the mineral water. It looked red-yellow and
had a fruity odor.

"That figures," said Joe. "Women like that perfume."
He looked at Martha as if he was sizing up a horse, then
turned back to Charley.

"So? What next?"

"First off, stay in your own stable."

"Sure, Chuck."

"Next, you tell me what happened."

"You moving into the house? On the other side?" Joe
nodded across the garden.

"Yeah. Me and Martha."

"It's kind of messed up since you've been there. The
carabinièri."

"You talk like they live there."

"For a while they did. Trying to get a lead on you."

"Did they leave happy?"

"Didn't find a thing. It kind of helped, your not having any papers.

"I got. The name's Charley Delmont."

"Yeah? Tell me about it."

"Charley Delmont, that's all you know. What did they ask you?"

Joe moved his chair, shrugged. "What's your name, what's your home, what's your who knows what. You know how they are."

"No, I don't," said Charley and smiled. "And then you said?"

"I told them you're a buddy of mine and the name's Charley."

"And?"

"And nothing. I told them to ask you when you came back, that I didn't know nothing from nothing."

"And that they had to believe."

"A real clown. A real funny clown."

"Tell me about my alibi. What did I do that night when they got the truck?"

"Simple," said Joe. He shifted in the chair and leaned on his arms. "You were in it."

"From one clown to another, Joe—"

"You were in it, hitching a ride. Vittore was driving, picked you up on the road. He recognized you and gave you a lift."

"Very good."

"Vittore is taking the rap. Two months for transporting stolen goods. Two months only because he was just the driver, had nothing to do with the goods."

"They believed that?"

"They found papers to prove it. Way bill and so forth."

Charley relaxed. "Good old Joe. When it comes to details, when it comes to comradeship and so forth—"

"Can it," Joe said and looked at Martha.

The other girl came out of the bedroom. She was older than Francesca, but not half as developed. She patted her hair, stood around for a while, and then asked Joe for a cigarette. He gave her one. Then he offered one to Martha, who took it and lit it herself.

"How about Fanny," said Charley. "Doesn't she get one?"

"Fanny doesn't smoke."

"Of course. She's too young."

"That's right," said Joe. "She's too young."

Then Joe lit a cigarette and when he exhaled he waved for Francesca to stand next to the chair.

"Look," said Charley, "if you're going to start that again—"

"Stay in your own stable." He had Francesca's hand and was playing with her fingers.

"Eenie meenie minie mo," said Charley and smiled at Joe like a father. Then he got up, nodded at Martha, and waited for her at the door.

"I'll show you across so you can find the house. I'll be back in an hour. Business. Okay?"

"Okay," she said, and they walked through the weeds and past the lemon trees that had grown much too bushy. After a while Charley came back and went down to the street. Joe sat at the kitchen table and played with Francesca's fingers. He was looking out the door, across the garden.

Chapter Eleven

WHEN CHARLEY REACHED the *gendarmeria* it was one-thirty, which in most of Southern Italy is an inviolate hour. Not even tourists have made much of a dent in the siesta custom, and those Italians who do business during the early afternoon don't like themselves much for doing it. The siesta does not apply to official establishments, such as the police. And they don't like themselves for having to disregard it.

Charley hadn't seen many police stations from the inside—he'd been lucky. But they all had the same look to him. Gray paint, green paint, or no paint was the uniform, with blond varnished or brown varnished furniture for decoration. Posters on wall boards didn't count for decoration. They were all drab blacks and whites.

"*Buon giorno,* gatekeeper," said Charley and watched the *carabinière* scramble around in his chair. He was in shirt sleeves, and without his Napoleonic hat which made him look like a farmer.

"*Buon giorno,*" said the policeman. He had a red welt on his forehead where he had been resting on the desk.

"I'm Charley," said Charley.

The policeman stretched and smiled back.

"I'm Giancarlo. I am happy to meet you."

They looked at each other for a while and then Charley shrugged. "Giancarlo, I'm sorry to interrupt your thoughts, but—"

"No matter, Charley. I was only sleeping."

They smiled some more and Charley thought he might leave. Nobody would mind, least of all Giancarlo. But it would only delay matters.

"Giancarlo, I'd like to see your *comandante.*"

That made it official, because Giancarlo sat up and adjusted his suspenders.

"And your business, Signor Charley?"

Charley leaned over the desk and whispered, "Just tell him they found Charley."

"Ah, a code!" Giancarlo said, and ran down the corridor.

61

He reappeared after a while and waved at Charley to come down the passage.

"He will see you," said Giancarlo. "It must be a matter of importance."

"True," said Charley and walked into the room of the *comandante*.

He was putting his tunic on and when he was done he looked twice his actual size. His belt was lying on a couch in the corner and there was a red welt on his left cheek. It had the small pattern of a weave in it.

"Ah!" said the *comandante*. "I am pleased you did not hesitate to come at even this hour. You have found Charley?"

"I have."

"Forgive me." The *comandante* bowed. "I'm Conrado Capurello—"

"Charmed," said Charley and he bowed too. "I'm Charley."

They both came up at the same time. Charley smiled. Capurello didn't. Then he smiled too and made a generous gesture.

"I will take your word for it, *signore*. You are under arrest."

Charley sat down and waited for Capurello to settle behind his desk.

"And I have come to make a complaint."

"Complaint," said the *comandante*. He was polite as before, but now it was business.

"I'm not complaining about my house, the way your *carabinieri* turned it into, into—what shall I say—"

"I understand."

"—and that it will cost me a thousand lire to hire a woman to restore my house—"

"It shall be considered in our charge."

"Charge?"

"Your complaint, *signore*."

"The harm you have done to my good name!"

"Precisely our charge, *signore*."

Charley cocked his head and waited. He too was very polite.

"You are charged with avoiding us, with suspicious duplicity in the use of your name, and with lack of papers."

"I'm here to satisfy you," said Charley.

"Your name then?"

"Just call me Charley."

"No more?"

"Not in front of me, *comandante*." Charley made a winning smile.

Capurello got up and stood under the ceiling fan. It made his fine hair flutter out at the sides.

"What do your friends call you?"

"Charley."

"And your enemies?"

"Charley. If they know what's good for them."

"Precisely my point, Charley. There is never a last name."

"Oh, well," said Charley, "it's pretty hard to pronounce in Italian."

"Please," said Capurello. "Just try me."

"Well—"

"I will tell it to you. Charley Palooka."

Charley sat back and laughed loud and long.

"How did I pronounce it, Signor Palooka?"

"Fine, just fine." Charley got out a pill and put it under his tongue. "Only one thing. That's not my name."

Capurello walked behind the desk, found the folder. He read, ". . . mostly known by the name of Charley. Two witnesses suggest the last name Palooka, though the suspect is not locally known to have used it . . ." Capurello put down the folder and looked up. "Tell me, Signor Palooka, do you own the *osteria* near the square where you live? What name are you using on the ownership papers?"

"You know Vittore?"

"The one who drove the truck with the contraband."

"He's the owner."

"Ah! But he is just your front!"

"He owns it. We run it for him. He owes us some money, other obligations, but he owns it. It says so in the files of the magistrate."

"Indeed. Under what name do you own your house?"

"My buddy owns it. Joe Lenken."

"Ah. Well, back to Palooka. We have discovered that you are the Charley Palooka who spent one month in the jail of Torino. For possession of black-market merchandise. Date, December, Nineteen Forty-four. Am I right?"

Charley shrugged and kept sucking on his pill. He said, "That was just a joke. You know, a funny name."

"I don't know, Signor Palooka."

"A comic-strip name. I just picked it, because it was a joke. You ever see American comics?"

"I have heard of them, thank you."

"That's why, *comandante*. Just a joke."

"It is not your own?"

"Do I look like a palooka?"

"I do not know what most Palookas—"

"Well, I don't. Anyway, that's all over and done with. Years ago. I took my rap and it's over and done with."

"However, since you admit having used a false name, there is that charge to be added!"

Charley smiled. "There was a different government then, *comandante*. I remember. They come and go."

Capurello got up and took a few steps back and forth. He was beginning to get the feeling that he was playing a parlor game.

"Let us be concrete," he said. "What is your real name, uh, Charley?"

"Oh well—"

"I know. Let us say this. You drive a car, Charley?"

"A beauty."

"Let me see your registration."

Charley pulled it out, showed it.

"Delmonte?"

"I told you," said Charley. "I told you about that trouble with pronouncing it. The name's Delmont."

"Very well. Delmonte, then."

"No. It's Delmont."

"Very well!"

Capurello drew himself up, picked at the folder on his desk.

"I would now like to see the rest of your credentials, Signor—Signor Charley. All you have." Charley showed him all he had, answered all the questions, until Capurello was all through. Capurello made his changes in the folder, shook Charley's hand, and carefully closed the door after him. It was 3:15, still the inviolate hour. He went back to the corner of the room where the couch was.

Chapter Twelve

GIANCARLO HAD SHIFTED in the meantime and—like his *comandante*—had the red welt on his cheek now. Charley walked by and waved at him to go back to sleep.

Charley Delmont. It was official now, hook, line and sinker. A tourist bus drove by when he got into the Bugatti and Charley waved at the faces behind the glass. Some of them waved back. He got his little box out, took out two pills, put the box in his pocket again. Then he started to toss the two aspirin like a juggler. He wasn't very good at it and when one of the pills fell into the street he threw the other one after it. Then he drove home. At the top of the stairs he cut across the garden because he wanted to see Martha.

She had fixed up the inside of the house. The place was swept, the three rooms were straightened, and she had made a fresh bed. He found her new clothes hanging in the big closet and Charley felt that she meant to stay. But the house was empty.

Charley went to the pump in the kitchen and sloshed water over his face. Then he sat on the veranda where the big Judas tree cut off the view to the bay. She'd gone shopping, most likely. There wasn't a scrap of food in the house. Charley took out an aspirin and sucked slowly. Perhaps he'd trim down the Judas tree so the bay would show—he got up, put his hands behind his back. His fingers made little snaps. Maybe he'd plan a vegetable garden; maybe next he'd forget who Martha was, the girl that had looked down from the top of the bridge and never gave him a straight answer when he asked her what she had seen. And she wasn't shopping, that was a cinch. What was she going to use for money?

Charley turned and went across the garden, and the weeds tore at his pants with little rasping thorns. He slowed down when he saw Joe's open kitchen door. Then he heard Joe. Joe was laughing out loud, with that bouncing-stone effect, and that bastard hardly ever laughed out loud. Before Charley got to the door he heard Martha,

65

and her voice had never sounded that harsh and that fast. It was a long sentence, a strong one, and what it boiled down to was "no."

Then Charley stood in the door. He leaned against the frame and rattled his box in one hand.

Francesca stood by the stove, the other girl was combing her hair where the mirror hung on the door, Martha was at the sink holding a broom, and Joe leaned on the table. He half sat on it, arms folded.

He turned his head to the door and looked. Then he said, "'Lo, Chuck."

Then Martha moved. "Charley," she said and came over. "You're back. I just returned the broom and the bucket. Have you seen the house, Charley? Let's go and—"

"I've seen it, Martha. Nice."

Then he looked back at Joe again. He walked into the kitchen making a slow sound on the stone floor. He stopped, kept smiling.

"You've got two, Joey. Why three? What can you do with three all at the same time?"

They looked at each other, and two guys standing at a bus stop couldn't have looked more casual. Joe held it for a while. He ran his tongue around his teeth.

"Nothing to it," he said.

Charley kept smiling, the way he'd done up in Delmont's room. He put the little box in his pocket and when next he moved there was a bony sound where his fist connected under Joe's chin. Joe's head snapped up and he clattered back across the table.

The damage wasn't much, not the way Joe figured it. He shook his head and scrambled up. Charley hadn't moved.

"Just to make you mad, Joe, else you don't fight good."

"Don't worry," said Joe and pushed his hand up against Charley's chest because he stood that close.

Charley ignored the push and stepped back. He looked at Martha and jerked his head for her to leave.

"Send out your brood mares, Joe."

"No need. This won't take long." Then his hand swung out, held fast to Charley's shirt front.

When Charley had been pulled close enough he gave Joe the knee, just lightly.

"Bastard—" Joe said, and let go.

"Send them out, Joe."

Joe wasn't listening. His loose mouth wasn't loose any more and he started to crouch.

"Bastard," he said again.

"I know," said Charley. "You don't like it when I don't call my shots. I fight to win, not to make an impression."

"Bastard. Yellow, no good—"

Charley's fist made a blur, and Joe pulled back. The fist caught air, but Joe was a stupid fighter. He thought there was nothing but fists, a fight was not a fight unless the fists did it and maybe a bear hug in the end to crack something. That's how he caught the foot in the chest, and being on the move back already he flew hard across the table. He came up on the other side, gasping for breath, but roaring. He meant to rush, saw Charley waiting for him, and changed his mind. He threw a chair, but that was nothing. Tossing Francesca out of the way he made a grab across the hearth, came up with a knife.

Charley waited for him.

Joe handled a knife the way a boxer handles his fists, so Charley waited. He dropped his jacket off and when the roundhouse came he caught the knife in the cloth, spun hard, and Joe's right hand was padded.

It took another three or four minutes. Joe got in a punch once, close to the heart but not quite close enough, and once his fingers jabbed up near Charley's eyes. But then his leg gimped out on him, his neck felt like it had been snapped, and when his stomach caved he rolled down to the floor and thought he'd choke on it.

The water helped. Francesca poured it from a bucket and the other one kept running back and forth between Joe and the sink carrying a glass. Then they stopped, because Charley told them to. He told them to heat water and get some towels ready.

Then Joe started to crawl.

"The other way," said Charley. "To the bedroom."

Joe turned around, crawled to the bedroom.

"Climb in bed," said Charley and Joe groaned hard trying to get up. Charley gave him a boost and watched Joe stretch himself as best he could. There wasn't a mark on him. He lay still because he couldn't move.

"Call Fanny in here," said Charley.

Joe called and when the girl was there Charley told her to take off Joe's clothes.

She did and never blinked when Joe groaned or made a jerk.

"Got the hot water?"

Francesca nodded.

"Bring it in. And the towels."

Martha stood in the door and watched the two girls prepare the compresses. They packed Joe where Charley told them and then they put a blanket over him.

"I'll call you when he's ready to be changed," said Charley. "And close the door, Martha."

He pulled up a chair and had an aspirin.

"Joe baby. You listening?"

Joe breathed hard but didn't talk.

"We don't have to discuss Martha any more, do we, Joe?"

Joe didn't answer.

"Do we, Joe?"

"Okay, okay, now beat it."

Charley crossed his legs and dipped the chair back.

"And so to business. Anything new since I crapped out on that gas deal?"

"Go to hell."

"Joey, I'm talking business. Who's going to pay for the doctor bills while you lie there, and for the expense I had while I was away, not to mention the added burden of—"

"Go to hell, Chuck. And hide someplace before I get up out of this bed. You got maybe a day, maybe half a day before—"

"Joey, I don't like you either."

"So you better—"

"But you and me, Joe buddy, we got to stick forever. Remember?"

Joe lay without moving so it didn't look as if he was thinking. For that matter it never looked as if he was thinking at any time, which was a mistake. Of late he had been thinking a lot about Charley. He was getting sick and tired thinking about it and pretty soon it would be time to move, to do something. He wanted Charley out. Next chance that came, Charley was out. He thought of the knife in the kitchen, and that it had been a mistake. He was glad he'd lost the knife—better than losing his head. No, the way Charley was going might take a little time, would be more complicated, but that's the way Joe thought of it. He was—and only he and Charley knew this—a very complicated thinker.

"Nothing's moved," said Joe. "Since that gas deal nothing big's been moving."

"That's good," said Charley. "Gives us more chance to operate when something big breaks."

"Ya," said Joe. "While I lie here and you with that small-time hoor. That's how something big's going to break."

"Joe, she's with me now, so don't talk about her any more. Hear, Joe?"

Joe thought he'd better answer. He nodded his head and said yes. The nodding made him wince.

Charley got up and leaned on the end of the bed.

"Ever hear of Bantam, Joe?"

Joe looked down and crinked his neck again. He looked up at the ceiling and said, "Yes."

"You ever hear about Bantam dealing locally?"

"Bantam is big stuff. He wouldn't deal with us."

"Bantam is small, Joe. He's on a salary from the States. The reason he wouldn't deal with us is because that isn't his job."

"That's what I meant," said Joe.

"The reason he's never dealt with anybody here is because nobody asked him."

"Why should he? He's getting paid for something else."

"Joe," said Charley, "you think he wouldn't want to make an extra buck if I asked him?"

Joe thought about it and saw what was coming. One of Charley's deals. One of those simple, easy deals, except that nobody else had tried it. Bantam and his contacts could be worth a mint and Charley was going to set it up. Then Joe would do the details, because they always worked it that way.

"He's going to talk to you?" said Joe.

"He will."

"I bet. He never even heard of us."

"Not you, but me. He's heard of Delmont."

Joe wished he knew more about Charley's new name. Bantam knew it? Joe lay still and let his mouth hang open.

"Delmont must be hot stuff."

"Sure I am," said Charley.

"The other one, I mean."

"He wasn't," said Charley. "But it's good enough for an in. Good enough to make Bantam feel a little safer. Total strangers rattle a guy like Bantam."

"Sure," said Joe because he was hoping to hear more.

"That's it, Joe. All I got to do is find him."

"Ask around," said Joe.

"You ask around. I'm leaving for two days. You ask around and when I'm back you tell me."

"Sure," said Joe and Charley left the room.

As soon as he came out, Joe's two women came rushing through the door. He let them pass and forgot all about telling them to change the compresses.

Chapter Thirteen

MARTHA HAD CHANGED to a blouse and skirt which looked more like the local clothes. It felt more familiar to her and she looked good.

"Charley," she said. "I almost didn't wait any longer. What happened in the room?"

"Just business."

"After you fought, in the kitchen?"

"You got to understand Joe and me. We got our own ways."

"You aren't friends."

"That's all right. He'll stay away from you."

Martha knew better, but she was hoping, like Charley did. He went to the bedroom and changed clothes. Martha sat on the bed to watch him.

"You know the Judas tree by the veranda?" she said. "If you trim it a little—"

"I know. We can make a view." He stuffed the shirt in his pants and picked a new seersucker jacket. The other one was torn from the knife. "When we come back," he said. "First we'll have a vacation."

"Again?" She smiled from the bed.

"I hardly know you yet." He had meant it just for a remark but it reminded him why she was here in the first place and that he still wasn't sure.

"I'm easy to know," she said. "There's nothing else," but she looked down.

He didn't see it, and if he had, he would only have misunderstood. He might have thought she was hiding something which wasn't true, but she felt that he didn't know her only because he hadn't yet tried. Perhaps he'll make love to me now, she thought, and then when he leaves the bed he'll not leave altogether, the way he did before. He leaves without wanting to know me, she thought. If Charley had known what she thought he would have understood, because it was true.

He put stuff in his pockets.

"Two days," he said. "We'll go to Castellamara di Stabia, at the other end of the bay."

"To take the baths?" she said. "There's nothing wrong with my blood." She laughed.

"I know. We'll just swim. And if you can't swim we just lie in the sand. I know a cove there—"

"I can't swim."

"Good," he said and they packed a few things for the short drive to the other end of the Bay of Naples.

They had a room with a small balcony whose iron-work bellied out like a bird cage, but they never sat on it or looked at it. They kept the jalousies closed so that the room was dim except for the sunlight laid out in strips on the carpet. It striped their bare legs when they got out of bed and if they stayed in the room long enough they could see it creep all over the bed and the flowered wall.

They stayed four days instead of two, but except for the first morning they never were in the room long enough to see the light move beyond the carpet. They had sweet coffee and rolls on their way through town, stopped to watch the dowagers on their way to the baths, and went to the beach. Mostly they stayed in the cove Charley had mentioned. It turned out that Martha really couldn't swim nor was she interested. Most of the time she lay on the sand, half asleep. There, even her love-making was lazy. It fit the heat, the slow waves, the big, dull, always blue sky. During the noon heat they walked back along the beach to the restaurant with the long terrace built into the water.

"Do Italians go here too?" asked Martha. She sipped her *aranciata* and looked at the other tables without raising her head.

"Go ahead, stare at them," said Charley. "It makes them feel different."

"Are they all from America?"

"The ones with Hawaiian skirts are."

"That group over there, they must be English," she said. "The way they wear tweeds in this weather."

"No. The English wear ducks. As soon as they get off their island and there's sunshine they wear ducks. The ones with the tweeds are German."

"I thought tweed comes from England," she said.

"Maybe. But the English don't cut it that way, with a belt around the middle."

Martha shook her head and kept worrying about the tweed in all that heat.

"Tweed is casual," he said. "They are on vacation, which means be casual."

They never talked about anything more weighty. At first Charley had tried bringing up the bridge again, but it got harder each time and more removed. The longer he was with Martha the less could he think of the dark woman he had seen on the bridge. He didn't forget it altogether, but made it a small doubt, somewhere in the back of his head. After a while it was hardly a doubt any more, just something he might remember, because it had happened. And not as if it had happened with Martha.

On the last day she wouldn't go back to the beach after they'd eaten.

"Let's stay here and talk," she said.

"Sure."

"Or let's go to the dock and watch the ships."

"We can—"

"Or let's go home," she said. "I want to."

They went home and opened the jalousie in front of the balcony, but by now the sun had moved so their side of the house was in shadow. She was glad there was no sun and for a while they sat by the open balcony door and talked about nothing.

"I itch," she said. She rubbed her back against the chair and ran her fingers through her hair.

"The salt," said Charley. He took her bare arm, held it to his mouth. "It's salt," he said again. "Did you ever taste warm salt?"

She laughed about it and rubbed her arm.

"You made it itch even more," she said.

"I have that effect," he said, and watched her get up. She took towel and bathrobe and went down the corridor to where the ornate bathroom was. When she came back her clothes were over her arm and she was wearing the bathrobe. He didn't know why she had taken the towel along because she was still wet.

"I changed my mind," she said. "I'll dry here, in the air from the balcony."

She sat naked on the blue and brown carpet and shook her hair, making a spray. She pressed the wet hair flat against her head so that it looked polished. Her black eyes showed very large in the small face now. Then she stretched and Charley saw her moist body the way he had never seen it before—that naked, and that much his.

"Ask me how many lire," she said.

"How many lire?"

"You will have to ask the owner," she said.

"He's keeping it." Then he got up because he wanted her. They went to the bed, where her wet hair made a large soaked spot on the pillow and the sheet under her back got moist and warm. And then they were together with a first-time violence and they stayed together because it would have been sinful to be apart.

Chapter Fourteen

THEY LEFT FOR NAPLES in the early morning because they wanted to drive along the bay before the sun was all the way up. The morning air was uncommonly clear, making Vesuvius look very close. As the sun came higher the wisp of smoke over the volcano's crater turned from gray to pink, and then white. They drove slowly because Naples wasn't far and it was very early. The sun was just over the mountains when Charley coasted along the Naples quay. They stopped at Zi' Teresa, which is the waterfront restaurant nobody wants to miss when in Naples, but at this hour it was almost empty. The round tables were moist from the morning air and where the sun warmed the table tops the marble was steaming. A waiter took their order as if he weren't sure they had really come.

"Are we the first?" said Martha.

"No. Some officers from the *Borgia* have been here. They sail in a few minutes."

"Those tourist ships. They don't horse around with their time tables," said Charley.

"They have to finish off Capri, Ischia, and Sorrento today. What is your order?"

Martha had the normal thing which was coffee with hot milk and *pane con burro*, and jam. Charley took a chance with the waiter's temper and asked for an American breakfast. The waiter looked pained but wrote down orange juice, scrambled eggs, toast and coffee without milk. It turned out all right except he brought an orange flavored soft drink instead of the juice. Martha drank it.

"This is what you eat every morning, in America?"

"Mostly."

"I will make you that kind of breakfast."

"You cook?"

"Very well, if it is not too complicated."

"It isn't. Even the coffee is less complicated than yours."

"Which coffee?"

"They only make one kind in America."

She couldn't believe it, but then she thought that would make cooking for him very simple.

"It is. You use cans."

While he finished breakfast he sent her inside where the restaurant had a magazine stand. He told her what to get and when she came back with two American women's magazines he read the ads to her.

"Soup? Here, in a can. Smoky flavor already added. Fruit, fish, peas, milk," and he showed her. "All in cans. You can also buy it fresh, but then you never know how it will taste."

They went through the magazines for a while and then left.

At the end of the stairs Martha turned left and Charley went right, to Joe's house. Before Charley got there Martha was back.

"I need some money, Charley. There is no food in the house."

"Just buy for yourself," he said. "I may have to leave for a day or so."

"I will make you lunch today," she said and took the money.

Joe was at the table. He had a glass of milk in one hand and a pencil in the other. A ledger was open in front of him.

The thin girl had a towel and was drying the dishes. Fanny was making beds.

"A fair morning to you," said Charley.

Joe looked up and said, "Hi."

"I see only Fanny and no-Fanny. You slowing down?"

Joe gave a sidelong look and turned back to the ledger.

"I don't know about me slowing down, but you better. You're spending too much dough and we're not selling so hot."

"What about the cognac?"

"Slow. The way the French are exporting and selling cheap, we don't have much edge left."

"And the stuff from Germany, that's moving, isn't it?"

"Like backwards. Who wears cloth like that in this climate?"

"Inland they do. Change the setup and push more of it inland."

Joe sat back and started tapping the pencil.

"Look, don't tell me my operations when you're not doing any operating yourself, Chuck. Except maybe—"

"Joey," he interrupted. "I don't take your crap, Joey."

Joe shrugged but it didn't go away. The tension—a sly, quiet kind—had been there from the start, and neither Charley's light jokes nor Joe's indifferent face ever got rid of it. Charley sat down at the table but they didn't look at each other.

"You find Bantam?" said Charley.

"I found Bantam two days ago, when you—"

"Shut your lousy mouth, Joe. Just answer me what I ask."

The silence got worse.

"So where is he?"

"Genoa. You go to the San Giorgio, right by the railroad station, and ask for Signor Faldotte. If you're going to see Bantam it's through that Faldotte guy."

"That's all?"

"That's all I could get."

"How about Bantam's place? You find out—"

"Through Faldotte. Bantam moves a lot, but right now he's in Genoa. And I don't know for how long," he added.

They stared at each other for a moment but neither of them held it. As if they were hoping it would pass or as if they weren't ready to make it worse.

"I'll be gone two days," said Charley.

"Go ahead. Just don't come back without a deal. Nothing's been moving much—"

"I'm leaving Martha."

"Go ahead. I got my own."

"I'm leaving Martha because I don't mix women with business and I don't want you—"

"Yeah, yeah, I know."

"Just don't forget."

Joe looked annoyed. It made him squint his eyes and rub one hand on the table.

"So lay off already." Then he got mean. "And maybe give her a speech. She didn't look like no virgin to me, coming in here."

"Just don't forget," said Charley. He got up and put his hands in his pockets. "And so you have no doubts, Joe, I trust her. If you make a grab for her, Joe, I trust her to kill you," and he walked out.

He went down the steps to the street and walked to the *osteria*. He sent a man to get the Bugatti ready for the trip, then went to the basement room to get money out of the safe. There wasn't much, as Joe had said, but Charley wasn't too worried. He figured the Bantam contact could be worth a lot and no reason it shouldn't work. Then he went back to the house.

Martha was wearing the loose kind of thing she seemed to favor except that it was not dark, the way he had met her, but white linen and a blue and yellow print. She was in the big room, the kitchen, and both the hearth and the hot plate were going.

"I made you lunch," she said.

There was lukewarm coffee left in a cup and he drank that.

"Looks fancy," he said but he wasn't looking. He could have eaten on the road. He would have liked spending the time before leaving some other way. He'd had an idea she'd sit on the veranda while he clipped the Judas tree for a better view. She would sit there and tell him where to clip.

"Don't drink that coffee," she said. "It will spoil your appetite."

"It won't," he said. "If anything could this coffee might do it, but it won't. What kind of coffee is it?"

"That's how we made it at home."

"Terrible."

She laughed. "I know. It is terrible." She put plates on the table. "But you will like the food."

"Home cooking?" he asked.

But she misunderstood the word because there is no real word for it in Italian. She said, "No, we never cooked this at home."

"Something exotic, then," he said, because when she dished out the food he couldn't tell what it was.

"It will be familiar to you. My surprise," she said, and they sat down and ate.

He was surprised, but he didn't recognize it. He thought he recognized something—tomato soup, maybe, sugar, fish, milk. A thick cream sauce kept everything secret. And then he bit on a nut.

"Nuts, for chrissakes," he said.

"Do you like it?"

"For chrissakes—"

"Is it familiar?"

She looked expectant. Charley put down his fork.

"Look, Martha. What is it?"

"I thought you would know!"

He sighed, looked patient.

"Honey, if it's baby food, I'm glad I'm no baby. If it's food, tell me what kind."

She looked disappointed, because she had been sure he would recognize it.

· "You don't like it," she said. "I made you an American dish, Charley."

"A what?"

"From the magazine, Charley. The recipe is from one of the magazines for American women."

"Oh, no!" he said.

"There is tuna fish, walnuts, peas, soft bread—"

"Oh, no!" he said.

She showed him the recipe, a full-page spread with a color montage showing the housewife who looked all apron and pretty dress straight from the store window and half a dozen cans with arrows pointing into a pyrex pot so the reader wouldn't miss what it was all about.

"She is cooking it," said Martha.

"I know. But you don't see her eating it."

"It is no good?"

"Christ, Martha. Be honest—"

She laughed, throwing her head back. Then she picked up the plates and took them away. Charley got out the long bread, some sausage, and Martha cut up a head of lettuce. Then they had salad and the other stuff. When they were through he told her he was leaving for two days and she should fix up the house if she wanted, any way she wanted. Then he gave her some money.

"How many lire?" she asked.

"Ask the owner," he said. "The place is yours."

Driving along the Via Carilina, the inland highway leading north, he kept thinking about Martha in the house, how she looked on the couch under the overgrown window, and how she waved at him because he had told her to stay there and sleep.

Chapter Fifteen

CHARLEY SNAKED HIS WAY across the big foyer of the San Giorgio and stopped near the desk. Then he tried for the desk clerk. Italians don't often make a queue so it took some doing to get to him. It took fifteen minutes.

"Signor Faldotte, please."

"Room Two Hundred."

The man who opened the door was round and friendly. He waved Charley into the room as if he had been waiting a long time and offered a glass of Vermouth.

"It always sounds more festive over a glass of wine," he said. "My name is Faldotte."

He was polite and did not ask Charley a thing.

"Be seated, *signore*. It will taste more festive," said Faldotte.

Charley sat down and held the glass.

"It smells festive," he said. Then he got up and bowed. "I am Charles Richard Delmont, or Delmonte, as you might prefer." Then they both sat down and smiled.

"Signor Faldotte, I am not allowed to drink, as our friend Signor Bantam will testify, so without offense allow me to simply hold this glass and enjoy it as your token of welcome and as a reminder of my more carefree past."

They talked a while longer like that and then Charley got tired of it.

"I am told you can help me find Signor Bantam."

Faldotte was tired of it too. He said, "Who told you?"

"Nobody told me. I know. I've known Bantam for over ten years."

"Then why come to me?"

"I've been abroad."

They smiled at each other.

"You are a friend?"

"Tell him Delmont. Delmont the drunk."

Faldotte smiled as if embarrassed and said, "Really, *signore*—"

"Just tell him."

Faldotte went to the phone and called. Then he turned back to Charley.

"He does not know you."

"Tell him the whorehouse in Milano. The drunken countryman, right after Bantam came to this country."

Faldotte talked to the phone, turned back.

"He remembers you but he sees no reason to meet you."

"Tell him I'm sober and it's blackmail. I'm here for blackmail."

It worked. The phone conversation was very short after that, and after Faldotte had hung up the receiver the door to the next room opened and Bantam came in. He had been next door all the time.

"You Delmont?" Bantam spoke English.

"The same."

Bantam came across the room with quick steps because he was short. His face was sour and he wore a tight collar.

"What's this crap?" He stood in front of Charley, a straight stance, because he was all pleated.

"Crap. That's all. Just wanted to get you out." Charley smiled.

Bantam and Faldotte looked at each other but neither of them knew what would come next. Bantam nodded and Faldotte left the room. Charley could hear him lean against the door outside.

Bantam had a pruny face and he kept sniffing his nose. He sat down, with precision, because he was all pleated.

"What is this?" he said.

"Do you remember me?"

"I remember Delmont. Who are you?"

"Delmont," and Charley tossed him a registration card. He also showed him his driver's license. Bantam gave them back and went to the door. He had a low conversation with Faldotte outside, then he came back.

"The reason I'm here—" said Charley but Bantam waved him off.

"Sit still and wait." Bantam stood by the window and looked out.

Charley waited. After a while he got up and talked across the room. "When you're through watching the pigeons give me a call. I'm in the same hotel." He went to the door.

"Just sit still," said Bantam.

When Charley looked back at him Bantam was still at

the window but he had turned. The black hole of his gun
was looking at Charley's stomach.

"You want me to sit?" said Charley.

"Yeah."

"I'll sit," and he did.

It took thirty minutes, and then the phone rang. Bantam waited a minute till Faldotte came in, gave him his
gun, and went into the other room to pick up the exten-
sion. Charley waited another five minutes and then Bantam came back. He sat down like before.

"When'd you get here, Delmont?"

"Today."

"I don't mean that."

"Oh," said Charley. "Maybe a week and a half ago.
Amir brought me."

Bantam sat still and sniffed.

"That's what Amir says," and he looked at the phone.
So far, fine. Charley kept smiling and waited.

"Amir says you were nothing but trouble."

Charley shrugged.

"And how come you're sober?"

"I been sober for years, Bantam. You just haven't
noticed."

"Amir says—"

"Screw Amir."

Bantam sniffed and wanted to say something but Charley cut him off.

"Something else Amir doesn't know. I've been in and
out of Cairo for the past five years, all the time he thought
I was rolling in some gutter or maybe selling his dirty
junk."

"He says you didn't sell so good."

"His percentage wasn't worth it, unless you took your
payment in trade. And I'm no hophead. I'm not even a
lush any more."

"Amir says—"

"I told you what you can do with Amir."

"So why'd you stick around?"

"You stick around Amir and you learn things, friend.
That's why I'm here."

"I don't get it."

"You will. Once you get off your horse and listen."

Bantam thought there was no harm in listening. Delmont was a rat, he remembered, just a small-time chiseler made harmless by the bottle. He hadn't thought of Delmont since the last time he'd seen him, the time Delmont was trying to sell him some whore. He had even forgotten what Delmont looked like—just that he was harmless and a big-talking drunk. Only Delmont wasn't talking big any more, and he didn't look like a lush. A man changes once he's off the bottle. Bantam took a glass of Vermouth. He drank it and said, "Ah." Then he said, "Want some, Delmont?"

"Thanks. I've had mine," and Bantam didn't see a thing that might have meant Charley wanted any.

"Tell me, Delmont, why'd you quit?"

"It was time, don't you think?"

"Maybe," said Bantam and offered Charley a cigarette. "Thanks. I don't smoke."

Bantam lit one for himself and blew out a thick cloud. "That's weird," he said. "A guy's got to have something, and a drunk yet—"

"Former drunk."

"Former drunk yet. They usually smoke all the time."

"I got these," said Charley and showed Bantam his box. He put two aspirin under his tongue and sucked them.

"Let's see your tongue," said Bantam.

Charley saw that Bantam knew his way around. He bent forward, stuck out his tongue. He lifted it up so Bantam could see the dark spot from the constant irritation. Then he sat back and smiled.

"Suspicious bastard, aren't you?"

Bantam nodded.

"And a dumb bastard on top of it," he said and watched Bantam sit up.

"Now that you're no lush no more, Delmont, don't take advantage."

Charley just smiled and looked at Faldotte.

"Would you mind, *signore,* and give me the privacy of this room with our friend Signor Bantam?"

"What's he say?" Bantam leaned forward.

"He asks," and Faldotte sounded polite, "whether I would leave the two of you alone."

"Precisely," said Charley. "It would make it more festive."

"Festive?"

"A private nicety between me and Signor Faldotte," said Charley. "Well?" and he looked from one to the other.

Bantam nodded and they watched Faldotte leave.

Charley sat back, dipped one leg over the other. "Now the reason you're dumb, Bantam, is the way you keep living within your means."

"If you got some crooked—"

"No, no. Nothing crooked, Bantam. Let me show you. You've been here about nine, ten years, right? And all you make is your salary, your stinking salary from the States."

"Look, Delmont. Now that you're no lush no more—"

"Yes, I know. All this time you got your contacts with the States you sit here, do your two-hour-a-day job, get your suit pressed, and maybe take in a house once a month."

Bantam got rèd in the face, and if Faldotte hadn't taken the gun along he might have yanked it out then just to impress. What got him worse than the truth of it was Charley's offhand touch and that crazy smile. If the bastard would at least laugh—

"So here's my thought, Bantam."

Bantam relaxed because the voice wasn't offhand any more.

"Since the last time you saw me I've made my way, like I tried telling you before. A buddy and me got a nice little restaurant down in Naples, all kosher and so forth, and we also work the black market. We're so good, Bantam, we got more market than supply. Think of it, Bantam."

"I'm thinking."

"Good. How'd you like to sell us some rare goods that only a smart cookie like you with smart connections like you can get a hold of?"

"Like what? An alphabet bomb, maybe?"

Charley laughed. "You're a wit, Bantam, but seeing I'm no lush any more you might try being serious. I've been making sense, haven't I?"

Bantam nodded. It made good sense. "Like what, Delmont?"

"Drugs."

"What drugs?"

"Never mind what drugs right now. First tell me can you deliver?"

Bantam got up and smoothed his pants. He sniffed a few times because he liked wasting time when he was sure. Then he said, "Me and the syndicate can get anything, Delmont. If you don't know that—"

"I know, Bantam, but you only handle stuff from here to the States. Can you handle it the other way around?"

"Listen, lush—"

"Ex-lush."

"Listen, Delmont, I can arrange for it to go straight up in the air and land on Mars or something. I can—"

"Good enough," said Charley. "That's good enough."

He liked dealing with Bantam. He had put a bug in Bantam's ear and Bantam could hear it buzz. It probably said money, money, money, and the sooner the better because after wasting ten years sitting around being errand boy—

"One thing, though, Bantam. I first gotta test your set-up."

"What's that?"

"What I'm after is pretty rare stuff, Bantam, and expensive. So let's first make a run that doesn't cost so much. And if something goes phlooey—"

"Suits me fine, Delmont." Bantam sounded aggressive. "And the same goes for you. What's your outfit?"

"We don't have a name. We don't wear bowling jackets that say Mott Street Musketeers or something. We just—"

"All right, save it. You operate from Naples?"

"Mostly."

"I'm coming down. Just to check around."

"Suit yourself, Bantam." Charley wrote down the address of their place and handed Bantam the paper. "Still think I'm small time, huh?"

"I don't know," said Bantam. "Depends on what you're buying."

"P.V.," said Charley and watched Bantam look ignorant.

"That's where we make the dough, Bantam. P.V. That's polio vaccine."

Bantam was impressed. He saw that Charley had vision. Bantam saw his income go up like a rocket.

"But first, Bantam, a test run. I want one five hundred carton of Aureomycin. Two weeks delivery. Can you make it?"

"I'll see. First I check your outfit and then we'll see."

"Set it up before coming down to Naples. That way we don't waste any time and you can always cancel."

"You'll get it. One case of Terramycin."

"No, Bantam. I want Aureomycin."

"All right, all right. We'll arrange it after Naples."

They both got up and Charley saw he had Bantam.

"One more thing, Bantam. Your percentage is going to be high, one-fourth, and I know nothing about your operation. You never did it before. So the first run will be on consignment."

"You crazy or something? I never—"

"You can do it, Bantam. You got the pull in the States, haven't you? And the standing?"

"Are you gentlemen—"

Then Faldotte came back into the room.

"We are," said Charley. He looked at Bantam and smiled. "On consignment." Then he looked at Faldotte and smiled. "Because seeing I'm no longer a lush and it's more festive this way."

Chapter Sixteen

THE FIRST DAY he left her alone. He saw her coming across the garden, saw her talk to Fanny and borrow something. Joe just nodded at her from where he sat, and let it go at that. He saw her again at night. He came back from the *osteria* late at night and saw her light at the end of the garden. He walked up a way and saw how Martha was sure that she was alone. She was behind the kitchen window, washing her blouse in the sink. She had just taken it off. Joe turned back and went to his house because he wasn't the kind that looked. He wasn't interested in just looking.

So he left her alone the first day, and the second day Charley called saying he'd come back tomorrow. So Joe took his time the second day.

He walked across just before noon and found her on the terrace.

"Fanny says she needs the soap and the bucket." He stayed where he was, one leg up on the terrace.

"Oh," she said. "It's you, Joe."

He just waited.

"I'll get them for you," she said and went into the house.

When she turned back to the door he stood there so she couldn't get out. But perhaps she was reading things into him. He looked bland enough, came toward her just to take the bucket and the cake of soap.

"If you need something else just drop around. One of the women will give it to you."

But it was exactly that blandness which made his presence so strong. That impersonal way of looking at her seemed to kill her identity, made her feel as if her body were not her own.

"Thank you," she said. "I won't need anything else before Charley comes back."

Joe turned at the door and said, "He called last night. He'll be back tomorrow."

"Not till tomorrow?"

"And he says to give you regards," he lied. He stopped

87

again on the terrace, looked at the Judas tree. "Tell him to cut that some. You get a nice view from here with that tree cut some."

She had been glad he was leaving, but when he delayed again to look at the tree it no longer felt like a delay.

"He will do that," said Martha. "We talked about it."

Joe made a short laugh. He leaned against one of the posts holding the arbor and swung the bucket against his leg.

"He'll be saying that for a while longer. You'll get used to it."

"Oh, no. We will do it when he comes back."

Joe laughed again and stopped swinging the bucket. He went to the end of the terrace.

"Come along across. I'll give you the shears."

He waited till she came and she followed him because that way he would leave her house.

He went through the kitchen and through the room behind and came back with the shears. He threw them on the table and sat down where he always did.

"Take them," he said. "That way he'll do it sooner."

She came to pick up the shears and he said, "Want some *aranciata?*"

He had left the door open and Martha could see his two women there. Fanny sat on the bed. She was leaning against the wall and looked at her legs in front of her. The other one was sewing something.

"Fanny," he called. "Bring Martha some *aranciata.*"

The bed creaked and Fanny got up. She put on one of Joe's shirts and came into the kitchen.

"Go ahead, drink it," said Joe and Martha sat down at the table where Fanny had put the glass. The noon heat had started to creep into the house. Martha sipped the cold drink and watched Fanny go back to the bed. Fanny took the shirt off and lay down on her stomach. She put her head to one side and looked at her hand.

"You give him the shears," said Joe. "He'll get around to it sooner."

"I will," said Martha. She fluffed her blouse in front because she was warm.

"You'll learn," said Joe, "when you know him longer. You known him long, Martha?"

"I met him in Rome," she said.

"You don't know him long." He had a spoon in his hand and started to make blunt lines on the soft pine table. "He pick you up in Rome?"

"I picked him up."

She smiled when she said it because she wanted their talk to be light and without meaning. She wanted to keep it that way because it might change Joe's tack. Where did you meet him, how did you meet him? he wanted to know, and next he would ask what did you see on the bridge, under the bridge—

"That's a new one," he said, and kept pressing lines.

She laughed again. She said, "He was sick, you know. He was bleeding." That way she hoped to talk about something else without seeming to.

"Oh, that," he said.

"Yes. At first I thought he was drunk—"

"Charley don't drink."

"Oh yes. He smelled from it."

Joe just sat for a while. She had told him something. Charley had taken a drink.

"So he was drunk," said Joe. "So he got sick from drinking too much and you picked him up." He laughed and said, "Very romantic."

Martha put down her glass and started to get up. Joe waved at her without bothering to look.

"Don't mind me. Drink your *aranciata.*"

She sat and felt foolish about getting offended. Joe didn't matter, or what he thought—except this wasn't true. He mattered because he was digging, trying like Charley had done to make her remember things which she may never have seen. And she would tell him something: she would tell him nothing.

"He had fallen down an embankment but it was the wound which had made him weak, not drinking."

"What embankment? The railroad?"

"By the Tiber. Near the bridge where I live."

"He was drunk, all right," said Joe, because he wanted Martha to make an objection. He would dig from there.

"But that isn't true. Because later he drove the car. He walked with pain but not drunkenly, and his thoughts were clear."

"Could be," said Joe. "Drink your *aranciata.*"

The bed creaked again because Francesca had turned on her back. She had her legs drawn up, holding her

hands around both knees. The other girl was through sewing. She and Francesca talked in low tones.

"He must have been muddy from head to foot," Joe
said suddenly. "Rolling down that embankment."

Martha had to think and she remembered that he
hadn't been muddy.

"Perhaps it was dry there," she said. "Perhaps he had
brushed himself off."

"Sure." Joe held the spoon and dug more. "So you've
been with him ever since, huh?"

She smiled and nodded.

"He phoned me from Rome, you know. He didn't
mention you though, the old bastard."

She smiled again.

"Because he must have called you before we met. I
was with him all the time after we met." She finished her
drink, held the glass in her hand. "Still, I don't think he
would have mentioned me. Not then."

"No?" Joe looked interested.

She got up to put the glass in the sink. She thought
she would change the subject and leave.

"He might have," she said, "because he was alone for
a while. I went shopping and he went to a bookstore."

Joe laughed hard this time, pushed his chair back.

"To a bookstore!"

"And why not?" she said. Then she tried to pass him.

"Because he don't read, not even the paper. What
bookstore was it?" He had stopped laughing.

"It was called Alivar's Bookstore, and we went there
twice!"

"A day or so later, to get another book?"

"Yes. A day or so later," she said and remembered that
Charley hadn't bought any books. But it didn't matter
to her because now she wanted to leave.

Joe let her pass. He didn't think she could tell him
much more. She had started to tell him the best right in
the beginning. She had said Charley was drunk, maybe
not drunk but he had been drinking. He had called up
Joe, stone sober, and when Charley had heard that the
carabinièri were chasing him, that's when the bastard had
suddenly started to switch. He had sounded hard and
he had said he was coming back just the same. With bells
on, he had said, and it sounded as if he had just made up
his mind. He had started to drink after that, maybe not

much, but even one shot with Charley meant something
extreme, something big—and it meant Charley was going to do it.

Next, he was under a bridge at the Tiber.

Next, that same night, he had kept the girl with him,
just like that.

Next, Alivar, the forger. And only a small job, maybe
a day or so.

And when he showed up in Naples, Charley had a name
good enough to go bragging with it to the police.

"Martha? Wait a second."

She turned outside the door. Joe hadn't followed her;
he was in the back room, by the bed.

"Martha?"

She came back in because Joe had sat down on the bed.
He didn't look as if he wanted anything from her, just
tell her something, perhaps.

"Bring us a glass of that stuff, willya, Martha? Fanny
wants a glass of that *aranciata*."

She thought she'd bring it to her. It was like Joe not
to get it himself and the other girl wasn't in sight. Martha poured a glassful from the cold bottle in the icebox
and went to the bed. Fanny sat up. That's when the door
went shut.

"I told Adele to close it," said Joe. The thin girl had
been behind the door. She was leaning against it now.

"May I have the—" Francesca started to say. She held
out one hand.

"Shut up," said Joe. It was off-hand and he never
stopped looking at Martha. He pushed Francesca back on
the bed so that it bounced. Francesca's flesh repeated the
movement. Then Joe reached for the glass, held it between
his knees.

"Look, Martha, relax." He watched her. She stood in
the room as if she were stone.

"What do you want?"

Joe made a bored sigh. He started to pat Francesca's
stomach, then he rubbed with his palm, counterclockwise.

"Don't act dumb," he said.

The small room felt suddenly clogged, clogged with
thick air, and with heat, with the girl on the bed who
looked like she was waiting to come awake, and Joe. Thick-
set Joe with his mouth closed now and his eyes as un-
troubled and sure as if Martha had already said yes. Or

as if it hardly mattered whether she said yes. Adele hadn't moved from the door. She leaned there looking curious.

"I don't want you," said Martha.

It surprised Joe when she said it but he had an answer. He even meant what he said.

"That don't matter. Take off your clothes." He sat, waiting for her to do it.

"Tell Adele to open the door."

Joe sighed again. He rubbed one hand through his hair and made an impatient gesture.

"Look, Martha. Don't act the nun. Ask any of them, ask Adele. Hey, Adele, you like it here?"

"Yes," said Adele. "I like it here."

"You see? She likes it. You'll like it. So come here."

Martha's eyes narrowed a moment, opened again. Adele was still by the door and all Joe had to do was lean forward a little, put down the glass, and touch her. Or he might take his time getting up, put the glass on the dresser, and then grab her around the waist. There was another bed, an empty one, and he would probably take her there. Nothing much showed in Martha's face. Then she pushed up her hair. She bit her lip just to make it moist.

"You mean now?" she said.

"Sure."

She smiled at him, cocked one hip slowly. "You must put the glass down," she said. "With one hand—"

"Don't worry." He swirled the orange liquid. "Get undressed."

Martha shrugged and looked down at herself. She sucked in her breath so Joe could see how her belly went flat, and unhooked the skirt. It fell to the floor. Martha stepped out of it, cocked her hip the other way, waited.

"The rest," said Joe.

There was just the blouse and Martha did it easily. She opened the top, pulled the blouse over her head. She was naked and ran her hands up her sides.

"This bed, Joe?" and she took small steps to the dresser next to the bed.

Joe watched her move but he wasn't the kind who looked long. He took a deep breath, got up, put the glass on the dresser. His big hands came down on her shoulders, lay there a while, moved slowly around her back. Francesca had turned back on her stomach and was looking at the crook of her arm. Adele sat and watched.

"Not so hard, Joe. My arm." Martha leaned her head back. She was smiling. "Let me have my arm," she said.

"Lift it," said Joe and watched her do it.

Then she reached past his side, where the dresser was. When she circled his back to pull him against her he hadn't noticed a thing till she poured. She poured the cold *aranciata* down his neck, doing it slowly and laughing into his face when he gasped. He let go fast and stepped back but when Martha kept laughing he started to laugh too and yanked at his shirt.

"A joker, huh?" and he laughed loud because he was still confused. "I finally got me a joker, huh?" and he yanked the shirt over his head.

When he saw Martha's face again it didn't make sense —till the glass broke. She did it so fast the first thing he saw was the jagged glass teeth of the rim and Martha holding it. She was breathing short breaths and seemed flushed all over.

"Yes, the joker. Here is the joker," she said and she talked so fast it came like a hiss. "Come, Joe, come reach. Touch the joker, Joe, touch me here, here, perhaps here."

His mouth came open, but he wasn't pretending. His white skin looked like a shiny maggot, a big maggot just peeled out of the egg, and he didn't move.

"You won't come, Joe? I come," she yelled, and didn't wait for his move.

The glass missed his face because he had jerked back in fright, so she had his neck. She didn't wait to see where the glass bit but slashed him the other way so a long streak came out red on the white chest, and back down over his arm when he stumbled and landed on Francesca. The girl pushed him away so she could turn and sit up. Martha had time then, because Joe was holding his neck with both hands, frantic because he thought the jugular might be cut. He yelled for Francesca to get off the bed, to bring water, Adele should bring bandages, bring a mirror—

Martha got dressed and shook back her hair. When Adele rushed in with the mirror and held it up for Joe, Martha walked over. She was not through being angry. She took the mirror away from Adele and broke it over the edge of the bed. Then she walked out. She went down the steps and walked along the streets for a while because she was still angry. She wondered how Joe would try it next time.

Chapter Seventeen

MARTHA WOKE UP, cold, before the morning light was really there and sat up with the blanket around her. The blanket was moist with dew, there was dew in her hair. She stretched a little and saw the house further down. Nobody was there. Turning, she saw the black kitchen door at the other end of the garden and it was still closed. Joe must be sleeping, she thought. He had probably slept all night.

Then she got up and came down the slope of the hill which ran into the garden. She hung the blanket up to dry, went into the house, took the knife out of her pocket and put it into the kitchen drawer. She drew water and set it to boil. She would drink some coffee. She would make it strong and then change her clothes, comb her hair, because Charley was coming. He would see her waiting and happy, really happy because she wanted him back. And that way he would never know about her night under the bush, up the hillside, and he would never know about the glass cutting Joe's throat before he could get to her. Joe wouldn't talk. He would have some explanation.

She had hoped Charley would come in the forenoon, early perhaps, so when she saw the movement across the weeds she ran for the knife again because it was too early. Then she saw it was Charley, and running out to him she almost forgot to leave the knife behind.

They met at the end of the veranda, and when they held each other Martha thought he might wonder about her, about the hard way she held him and pulled him close. But he didn't. He wasn't surprised, but held her the same way. He grinned at her and winked, like they had a secret, and the way they walked into the house together they might have been together for years. She made breakfast and forgot about the day before and the night she spent on the hill.

"In case you don't know," he said, "I'm glad to be back."

"Because I was waiting for you."

94

"Because I'm such a nice guy."

"I know it too," she said.

He drank the coffee and watched her smoke a cigarette.

"How was Joe. Any trouble?"

"No trouble," she said. She smoked. "But don't go away again, Charley."

He put his cup down and sat still for a moment. "What did he do?"

"Charley," she said, "believe me that he cannot do harm to me."

"You tell me if he does?"

"And I would ask your help."

Charley sipped from his cup and considered that she hadn't answered his question. It was a lot like the first time, asking her about the bridge and her answers always simple, straightforward, but without answering what he wanted to know.

Perhaps he didn't ask right—he knew he didn't ask the real question. He would have to say, "Did you see me dump a dead man in the river?" He was sure she would answer him, except then there would be no point asking the question. Then she would know—and he was no longer sure what he would do then. He didn't want to think about it and spoil everything.

And about Joe, he would have to ask, "Did the bastard put you in his stable?"

Charley got up to go to the sink. He washed his face with cold water and snorted through his fingers. Then he said, "Give me a towel, Martha." Except he felt sure she would have told him—or she wouldn't have stayed waiting for him. He rubbed his face and neck hard because it distracted him from the way he felt.

"Martha?"

"Yes, Charley."

"I'm going to see Joe. Business. Come along."

"I'm coming," she said and they went across the garden to the kitchen door.

The door was open now, but Joe wasn't at his table. Adele was at the table drinking hot coffee.

"Buon giorno," said Charley. "We'll have two of the same."

Adele always looked hostile so it didn't mean a thing to Charley.

"And get Joe," he said when he took the coffee.

But the door opened before Adele got there and Francesca came out. She carried soiled bandages which she threw into a pail under the sink. There was a half-eaten roll on the sink. Francesca picked it up and finished eating it.

"That's a trouper for you," said Charley. "How's the roll, Fanny?"

She didn't answer, because Joe came in. Except for the adhesive across his throat and the shirt buttoned with sleeves rolled down he looked the same.

"When'd you start shaving, Joe?" Charley cocked his head at him.

Joe sat down and Adele gave him a glass of milk.

"Kinda early, aren't you?"

"You're up," said Charley. "Or was it Fanny? Did Fanny scratch you? I always knew that girl had spunk. I kept telling myself one of these days Joe's going to try his funny business with that little girl, and she'll—"

Charley never noticed how everybody got still, waiting for him to finish and not make it worse. Then Joe interrupted him.

"Wasn't Fanny," he said. "Martha did it."

It seemed as if the silence before had been one big racket compared to now. Only Joe moved. He was scratching his ear. When Charley talked it sounded smooth, and he talked without turning.

"Martha," he said. "You cut him?"

"Tell him," said Joe.

Martha was learning fast about Joe. He wasn't dumb, and he wasn't simple.

"He's tricky," said Charley. "Let him tell it. Just sit still, Martha, and let him tell it."

Joe took a big swig of milk and sucked his lips.

"All right, Joe. And make it simple."

"It is simple. I tried laying her and she cut me."

"That all?"

"I didn't lay her, if that's what you mean."

Charley looked down and smiled to himself. He got out his box, pushed it back and forth on the table.

"That's what you told me, wasn't it, Martha? That you took care of it."

"Yes, Charley."

"You should have told me more, Martha. I don't like

hearing it from Joe." Charley wasn't looking at her.
"I thought this way—"

"I know, Martha," and he looked at her for the first
time. She looked back at him and he made her feel better.
Charley put the box back in his pocket.

"Just the throat?" he said.

"Like hell," said Joe. "And across here, and here."

"I'm disappointed. At least she should have cut off
your—"

"Look, Chuck—"

"Now she won't have a chance any more. Now—"

"Chuck."

Charley turned his eyes to Joe and shook his head.
"You don't think I'm through with you, do you, Joe?"

"I was hoping you were," said Joe. And then, "Why
do you think I told you? I could have told you a cock-
and-bull story easy. Couldn't I, Martha?"

"Don't talk to me. You filth."

Joe said to Charley, "Because I don't want it to go on.
Same reason Martha kept it the way she did. So it stops.
Sounds weird, doesn't it?"

"Sure does."

"But I'm telling you, Chuck." Joe chewed his lip. "You
know I never run into the likes of Martha before, you
know that? So I'm laying off. I'm telling you straight
so it ends here. Believe it or not."

"I don't know yet. You believe him, Martha?"

"I didn't expect him to talk about it," she said.

"But I did," said Joe. "Judge for yourself."

"Why, Joe?"

"I don't want to break up and I don't care for your
woman. That's all there's to it."

"Ah! This, our beautiful friendship."

"Friendship, crap. The business."

Charley looked back at Martha and neither of them
spoke for a while. He got out his box again, took a pill,
put the box back in his pocket.

"I'll make small pieces out of him, Martha. Business or
no business. What do you say, Martha?"

"Let it be, Charley. You will make it worse."

"Or at least if you had cut off—"

"Let it be, Charley."

"Okay," he said, "I'll let it be," and for the moment
he even thought it might work.

Martha was glad it stopped this way and hoped it would work. And Joe—he knew it had worked. He was glad there was time now, because he hadn't been ready. He didn't gamble often, and when he did he was after only the biggest. It had been that way when he gambled on changing from Corporal Lenkva to Lenken the citizen. He had won then, and he meant to get his this time. It looked pretty good because nobody knew that Lenken was gambling, which showed just how smart he was.

"So talk business," said Joe. "About Bantam."

Charley nodded at Martha and she left. He looked after her until she disappeared in the garden.

"Send them out," said Charley, and this time Joe didn't argue. Francesca went into the bedroom and Adele went down to the street.

"Bantam is coming here in a day or so. Then we make a deal."

Joe nodded as if he were thinking. He said, "Why here? You couldn't—"

"Because he wants to, that's why."

Charley felt irritable and wanted to get away. Nothing had happened in the meantime to make him feel less sure but that's how he felt. Less sure about Joe, and edgy. He had listened to Martha and let it go. He got up.

"Stay a sec," said Joe. "I gotta know more."

"All right. Bantam wears pressed suits and is interested. What more?"

"He'll do business?"

"Looks so. He wants to check that we exist and it isn't a trap. He wants to look at you, my partner. Okay?"

"Fine," said Joe. "You must have snowed him good. How'd you do it, Chuck? He knew Delmont?"

"You're awful talky today, Joe buddy. What's come over you all of a sudden? You got an idea maybe—"

"I gotta know, don't I?"

Joe was right. Charley was anxious to get away, he was sick of Lenken and knew it would get worse the longer he stayed. It had even made him forget about telling Joe what to say to Bantam.

"He'll want to know about me. Tell him you've known me for maybe ten years and I used to be a lush. I stopped five years ago. I used to be a lush but not any more. Most of the time I've been here in Naples, but off and on for the past five I've been shuffling between here and

Cairo. You don't know much about that except it was Cairo. Clear?"

"I got it. It's got to do with Delmont."

"I'm Delmont and all I'm telling you is what I told Bantam. So don't slip."

"Bantam must have known Delmont," said Joe, as if he hadn't been interrupted. "How come Bantam took you for Delmont?"

"Because I reminded him and because I didn't stick out my stupid neck." Charley got up, kicked the bench out of the way. "If you get what I mean," he said and walked out.

Joe watched him leave because he didn't want any more. It had been a small question and he got his answer. Delmont knew Bantam once. That's all Joe wanted to know. Now he just waited for Bantam.

Chapter Eighteen

WHEN CHARLEY WALKED up the terrace he saw the Judas tree and remembered about trimming it. He stood a while and looked at the tangle but it didn't distract him. He felt more irritated. It got worse because there was nothing to think about, nothing to fix his uneasiness. There was Bantam, but that didn't worry him. Charley had done it well and he knew the deal was going to work. There was Joe. Right now that was settled and Charley was sure Joe wouldn't make a move, not right now, not before the Bantam deal was in the bag. If Joe meant to move, it wasn't going to be until later. But that didn't worry Charley because he was going to fix the first move himself. That left Martha to think about, but he hardly did. It felt strange to know this with so much certainty, but the only thing between him and Martha was something good.

"You've been standing there," she said. She put her arms around him from behind, and held him. "Were you thinking about trimming the tree?"

"Yeah. I want to trim that tree. It's crawling all over."

"Then trim it," she said.

"Ya."

She let go and came around to the front.

"Look at me, Charley. Are you worried about this Joe?"

"I don't know."

"I too think this may not be the end, Charley. But he is slow—not like you, Charley. And he is not like you because there is nothing straight about him." She put her hands over his shoulders. "So you see, Charley, if he wants me he will not try it again, not the same way. And I don't think he wants me, Charley. He is after you."

"You see fast."

"I pay more attention, Charley. Not like you." She tugged at his neck to make him look down at her and he saw her smiling. He put his hands on her waist and smiled back.

"Let's take a walk," he said. "I'll buy you some sweets."

"Monte Bianco?" she said.

100

"We don't have *Monte Bianco* up here. We got *pasticce-ria*, though."

"Get me some," she said. "And tell me what kind of *pasticceria*."

"It's terrible. Not just cake, you know, but with spice, candied orange peel, barley. And, naturally, cream."

"Ah!" she said.

"You can have two."

"Ah, ah!" she said.

They walked past the square and up the hill to the *osteria*. Charley started to talk about nonsense, laughed with her, and told her if she could eat three *pasticceria* he'd give her the baker for a present.

"How old is he?" she asked.

"Forty-five."

"I will take him."

"He is a woman and weighs three hundred pounds."

She said, "No, thank you, I will take something else."

"Take me."

"I have you. I will take your Bugatti."

When they passed the back of the *osteria* she saw Charley's Bugatti there and walked up to look at it.

"And you will have to teach me to drive it," she said.

"Never. You can never eat three *pasticceria*."

She patted the hood of the low car as if it were a dog and walked to the basement stairs.

"Your *osteria* is underground?"

"No, just the basement. Walk through. You'll come up at the other side."

Silvestro wasn't upstairs yet, singing shepherd songs, so the basement was quiet.

"What a shiny lock," she said and looked at the closed door. "Your storeroom?"

"No. Conference room. Joe and me talk business here."

"How do we get upstairs? I have business with three *pasticceria*."

They went upstairs and Martha ate two of them. "So you may keep your beautiful car," she said and wrapped the third one in a napkin to take it along.

First they walked uphill a way because that way the home trip would be easier. When the orchards started they turned back and went downhill till the street crossed a bridge. The bridge was narrow and arched over a gorge full of stones and dry eucalyptus trees. The road there hadn't been a street for so long it had become an over-grown path between orchards and broken stone houses. No-body lived there any more, just lizards.

"Where does the bridge go?" she asked.

"No place, really, except kids use it for a short cut down to the city. Come here. In the middle. Up there you can see Vesuvius, and opposite, the bay. Nice sight?"

They stayed for a while and then walked back. It was after twelve. The strong heat was pouring from the sky and everything held still under it. They thought about their cool house with the large cool bed where they would lie down and wait till the sun went lower.

When they saw the terrace they saw Joe standing there. He was leaning against the wall and had a twig in his mouth. Then he spat it out.

"Bantam is here," he said.

Chapter Nineteen

IT WASN'T A LAZY NOON any more, or a time to lie in the dark room. Charley nodded at Joe, who pushed away from the wall, and they left. Martha watched them go through the weeds.

"Boy, you pick 'em. You know how to pick 'em," said Joe. "A sonofabitch in pressed pants who comes around at the height of the day—"

"How long's he been here?"

"Snooping around the place, asking questions at the *osteria,* even at the docks—"

"Stop beefing."

They got to Joe's kitchen and Bantam was there, at the table. Joe gave him a dirty look. He yelled at Francesca to get him a can of beer and after she brought it he sent her out. Adele had already left. That was something new —Joe sending the women out and nobody had to press him, Joe being irritable and letting it show.

"Hi, Bantam." Charley sat down.

"Delmont," said Bantam. He had a glass of water in his hand and kept sipping from it. He waited for Joe to sit, but Joe stayed by the hearth looking gruff.

"You met my partner, I guess." Charley nodded at the hearth.

Bantam made his face go sour and didn't look at Joe.

"You know, Delmont, if there's going to be any deal around here, if something's going to shape up, that ox you got for a partner better learn to cooperate."

Charley looked over at Joe and couldn't figure it. Why should Joe try to queer this deal—unless Bantam was exaggerating.

"I haven't heard a thing about a deal," said Joe. He came to the table, banged his beer can down so it slopped. "This nobody—"

Bantam jerked around and glared.

"—he comes around here with nothing but questions, snooping around and stirring up who knows what trouble. Hell, he even tells me he sent a man to the magistrate's office to check on who we are! What in hell—"

103

"Shut up, Joe." Charley looked annoyed because he couldn't figure it. "Just shut up."

And as if he had made his point Joe didn't say any more. He sat down and held the beer.

"I told you in Genoa—" said Bantam.

"All right, forget it. Forget Lenken and remember you're dealing with me."

"I'm not going to sit here—" Bantam started again when the heat got Charley, or something got him and he slapped his hand on the table.

"You want to deal or we go someplace else, Bantam? Make up your mind." He was sharp and he meant it, because he could tell Bantam was gassing and nothing else.

Nobody answered. They were waiting for Charley.

"All right, Bantam. You came here to do a job. Did you find out what you wanted?"

"I found out."

"So come on, how's it look. We look good enough?"

"I checked around," said Bantam, not wanting to commit himself. "I made some phone calls after you left Genoa and checked around here." He sniffed. "Looks okay," he said, as if it were an effort. Then he jerked his head at Joe. "Except with an attitude like that—"

"Listen to me, Bantam." Charley leaned across the table. "You start getting coy with us and we throw you out. I can't use some small-time chiseler who gets offended when some stupid ass like Lenken here doesn't have the right manners. I can't use a punk who can't stick to business he's so sensitive with personal feelings. I'm telling you straight, Bantam—either talk business or don't talk at all. Office politics don't make a dent around here. Got that straight?"

Joe's mouth had come open, and he wasn't putting it on. The way Charley handled it was something to see; it was something to learn. He figured Charley must have gauged Bantam pretty close to push him around the way he did, because Charley never threw his weight except for a purpose. Then he saw that Charley had gauged it right.

"You can stop tearing my heart, Delmont. Or we don't deal."

That's the way Bantam put it, but it meant he was anxious and he was ready.

"So let's deal. You got it set up for one five-hundred carton?"

"All set," said Bantam.

"What did you get?"

"You said Aureomycin."

"That's what I said. And it's full potency. I have that checked, in case you—"

"It's the real thing."

"Where'd you get it?"

"Now look, Delmont—"

"You look. You tell me from where because I'm going to check how well you covered. I don't buy what leaves a track straight to my front door."

"It's from European Relief, consigned here."

"Port of Genoa?"

"Of course."

"That's where you arranged for it?"

"What else, Delmont. You think—"

"From now on we take only merchandise arranged for at the loading point. That's New York. That way they don't catch the theft by just checking the bill of lading. You got that, Bantam? I want to be covered all the way."

Bantam saw it and felt respect. But he covered it.

"You keep criticizing like that, Delmont, maybe you better go it alone. You said delivery in two weeks and I got it for you in just two days. That's nothing, maybe?"

"That's good enough to show you're eager. Where is the stuff now?"

"In Capri. There's a yawl in the harbor there—"

"Boy. You are eager."

Bantam gave Charley a dirty look and pushed his glass away. Then he looked at Joe.

"How about some of that beer, Lenken?"

"Get some," said Charley, and Joe did. He brought the beer and didn't say a word. While Bantam poured from the can Charley took his box from his pocket and rattled it. He thought the thing had shaped up fine, the merchandise ready and waiting just across the bay, Bantam so eager that he rushed it down ahead of time, and all on consignment. They could use it. Unless Bantam had rushed it too much, leaving a trail. Not likely. Not an old-time hood like Bantam—Charley could check that a little, make some calls to Genoa.

"Bantam, how come a yawl got here so fast, all the way from Genoa? You send it out a week before I came to see you about it?"

"Jerk," said Bantam and drank beer. "I brought it down in my car. The yawl picked it up just outside Naples."

"I like that, Bantam," and Charley smiled at him. He didn't grudge a man's being smart.

They talked details for a while longer, instructions to be phoned to the man who was waiting in the Capri restaurant, and then Charley got up.

"I'm going down to the quay. Set up the second haul," he said to Joe, "and get a delivery routine worked out. Sort of the same way we handled the French imports. Only twice as good."

"You're fixing a pickup for tonight?" said Joe.

"Tonight. I'm going myself."

"Go ahead," said Joe. "I'll finish up here. I'll phone Capri later."

Joe tossed his empty can under the sink and looked out the door to see which way Charley was going. Charley was cutting across the garden. He was going to his house first. And a while later he would come back this way to go down to the street.

Because of the trees outside and the closed wooden shutters, Charley had to wait to get used to the change in light. It was cool inside and the overgrown windows gave the dim light a green cast. He could hear Martha sit up in the other room. She had been asleep.

"Charley?"

He walked to the couch and sat down. Her shoes were off and she was wearing a cotton shirt.

"How you keep your belly so flat with all those sweets you keep eating—"

"I'm very active. All through siesta I toss and turn in my sleep." Then she stopped smiling at him. "You are leaving, Charley?"

"Ya. Just for the night." He got up and went to the closet. He still had the gun there, the one from Rome. "Just this night, Martha, and Joe won't be here. But take the gun. You know how it works?"

"No," she said.

"Here. Pull on this trigger and hold fast. That's all. And always remember, use it only from close up. The closer the better."

She nodded and watched him put it on the table. She

would use it; she would have no hesitation if it became necessary.

But they both felt how the gun didn't make his leaving easier. Leaving was no longer a one-night routine to do a fast piece of business—to make the island run that would take perhaps two hours or so. They felt the difference but didn't say anything.

"You seen my spray jacket? That rubber thing I had hanging here?"

"In the other closet, Charley, outside. It made a smell here so I thought—"

"That's all right. It does. We should always keep it out there."

He found the jacket and put it on the table. Then she watched him get canvas shoes with rubber soles and he put those on. He also took a long flashlight and put that next to the spray jacket, on the table. There was nothing else to do. He had everything, but he didn't want to leave.

"Look, Martha—"

"Come here, Charley." He came to sit by her and she leaned against him. "It is a bad time to think, Charley. You will do what is right, but now—" She didn't finish. His need for her had come with a suddenness that made him press her against him as if there were nothing else he could do. There was nothing else. It was the only kind of togetherness they knew. It was like a struggle, with the strength of just one more time each time, and it made them one.

When he left he kissed her good-by, leaving her quiet and almost asleep.

Chapter Twenty

JOE SAW HIM LEAVE. He had been watching for it. When Charley had turned to go down the steps Joe stopped watching. He slapped his hands on the table and got up. He wanted another beer.

Martha, too, watched him leave. She had gotten up when she heard Charley close the door and she came out to walk through the bushes that grew along the wall going down to the street. At the bottom of the stairs Charley turned back and saw her. He waved and Martha waved back. Then she sat on the wall where she could see the bay.

Joe came back from the icebox and put two cans of beer on the table. He said, "Take one," and pushed it over to Bantam. Then he sat down. He watched Bantam's face. Bantam didn't want the beer. He wanted to leave.

"Take it," said Joe.

Bantam got up. "You take it, Lenken. I got better things to do than hang around here."

"We're done. All fixed up the way Chuck wants it."

"That's why I'm leaving." Bantam picked up some papers and his pen.

"You got me wrong," said Joe. "I didn't mean any harm before."

It stopped Bantam but the look he gave Joe wasn't friendly.

"Listen to me, farmer. I'm older than you and I've been busy for longer than you. I left small time when you were maybe just starting to steal apples somewhere. I'm telling you just so you get your bearings. Don't horse with me, Lenken, because your type I'd just as soon see dead."

"Don't talk big, Bantam," but Joe saw it didn't upset the man.

"Like your friend Delmont said, we do business and leave out personalities. I've taken your crap for that reason. So stay out of my way."

"Well," said Joe, "I got more business."

Bantam laughed.

"Take it to the neighborhood gang."

"There's money in it," said Joe.

"Lenken." Bantam leaned close so Joe could see the skin of his old face. "You maybe think I'm a small operator, and I am, Lenken. But in a big organization. I can clap my hands and you don't eat breakfast tomorrow." Bantam went to the door. "Because of no stomach," he added and started to walk out.

Joe wasn't doubting a word of it.

"That's why I wanted to talk to you," and the way he said it, Bantam stopped, turned back toward the table. "I'm sorry about before. That was an act," said Joe.

"I don't get it."

"So come here and I tell you."

Bantam waited.

"Sit down, Bantam, and I tell you the rest." Joe watched Bantam stand there and saw he was interested. "An act," he said, "to make Chuck think I got no use for you."

Bantam sat down.

"So now I can talk to you, Bantam, and Chuck would never guess that you and I could do business together."

"What is it?" said Bantam. "The double cross?"

"It's murder."

"Wrong man," said Bantam and got up again. "I don't hire out."

"Wait." They looked at each other and then Joe went on, "Not even if it's your own skin?" When Bantam sat down again he pulled a cigarette out and lit it. Then he leaned into his chair, eyes blank, and smoked.

"You better tell me, Lenken."

"I will. How long have you known Delmont?"

"I never did. Just met him a few times."

"Quite a lush, that Delmont, getting off the stuff after twenty years, running a business like ours, being in Cairo and Naples all at the same time—"

"Talk plain, Lenken."

"I will, Bantam. But tell me, what does a guy like you—with your training and so forth—what does a guy like you do when he's roped in on a lie, when he's pushed around, and all the time the guy who does it is pulling a fast one?"

"You know the score, Lenken, don't you?"

Joe laughed. When he stopped he said, "Delmont is dead. This guy Charley is somebody else."

There was a silence while Bantam held the smoke in his

lungs and his face went stiff. If they got wind of this in
the States, Bantam getting himself sucked into a deal by a
guy he thought was somebody else—

"Who is he?"

"A guy I've known for fifteen years. He's not a cop,
if that's what you're worried about, but cops at least you
can go by." Joe paused. "You always know what they'll
do, they even wear uniforms so you can spot them—"

"And this Charley?"

"Figure it out yourself. He snowed you, didn't he?"

"Maybe you're snowing me."

Joe shrugged. "He's been in Cairo? Somebody there
must know what he looks like."

Bantam thought for a while and wondered why Joe was
telling him this. They weren't friends, that's for sure, but
why bring in an outsider, even risk ruining the business
deal they had on?

"How come he's alive?" said Bantam. "How come for
fifteen years you don't do the job yourself?"

"Because he's got me, Bantam. Something goes wrong
and it gets back to me I'm finished. I'm not set up like
you, Bantam. I haven't got the connections and all, and
with you doing this job I've got an expert on it."

"I told you, Lenken—"

"Wait. Think of it this way. Without Chuck what
have we got? A nice business with just you and me. He's
giving you twenty-five percent? You can make it fifty.
You ship the stuff in, I distribute; you cut out this guy
you don't even know, and I do business with a guy I can
trust. You and me, Bantam—"

"Shut up a minute."

"I'll shut up, Bantam; but remember, he's making the
pickup tonight, with nobody looking but your two men—"

When Bantam ground out his cigarette, Joe knew he
had him. Joe knew he had found the setup where Charley
was getting his and Joe wasn't even in it. He didn't know
where it would happen, who was doing the job; all he
knew was it was going to happen, and he'd end up with
a business layout much better than he had even dreamed.
He had to smile to himself because it left just one loose
end, like an extra bonanza. There was Martha.

"All right," said Bantam. "I'll check."

It was a disappointment to Joe, but he understood
about checking. Only it had to be fast.

"Check what? My story?"

"Like you said. Cairo. Ask them about this lush Delmont, if he ever left the town, how he looked, about that aspirin habit—"

"But you gotta do it now, Bantam, or we miss our chance. We can't—"

"You got a phone?"

"At the restaurant. Call Cairo, and then your hoods."

"All right," said Bantam. "If the Cairo call checks with your story, I'm in."

They looked at each other, each hoping the other wouldn't say something else to make this thing less simple or to upset the decision. When they heard the steps outside it was like a relief, no matter what might walk in.

Adele came through the door, and then Francesca. They stopped when they saw the two men and moved to leave.

"Come on in," said Joe, but they still hesitated. They had never seen him so animated, with arms waving and a grin on his face. "Come in already." He got up. When Francesca came by he slapped her rear and told her to cook something good for later. Then he looked at Adele. He was grinning.

"Pack your stuff," he said.

She didn't understand.

"Pack up and blow. I got a replacement coming. Blow, don't you hear?"

When he walked out the door he had one arm around Bantam's shoulder and that's how Martha saw the two men walk to the steps.

She saw them with the light slanting low now and Joe squinting his eyes because he was facing the bay where the sun was and he was laughing. He leaned close to Bantam and Martha saw Bantam nod while Joe acted as if he were telling a joke. She didn't hear what they said.

Martha got up from the wall and stood still so the bushes hid her. The low sun made a warm, friendly glow on everything, but Martha felt cold. Fear was a physical presence that squeezed her ribs, pressing her arms to her side. If Charley were here he could tell her, he could push it away and tell her he was back with her now and nothing to fear any more. But he wasn't. There was only the evil she felt coming from down below, where Bantam and Joe walked down the steps and turned toward the square. Even with Charley not here—if at least she knew where he was. Bantam would know, and Joe, laughing down the street. She ran back to the house because she had almost called out and was afraid to do it.

At first she tried to work in the kitchen, and then she thought it might help to sleep. She lay down, got up again. She walked out to the veranda and considered the Judas tree. Perhaps she could trim it. Back in the house she tried working again, but after a while it got worse. When she saw her scarf she took it down from the hook, draped it over her head and then, on the street, she looked like every other woman who might be hurrying to meet somebody.

She did not need to think, but walked to the *osteria*. That's where they would be going and from there, perhaps, to meet Charley. She would ask them. Except for an old man sniffing his wine, and a girl who was cleaning the espresso machine, the *osteria* was empty. They should be here; she had seen them turn into the place. The basement? Charley had said they had a room down there in order to talk. In the hall to the back was a telephone and when she passed it the bell rang. She took the receiver and said, "Yes?"

"Did you complete your call?" said the voice.

"Did I—"

"Did you complete your call?"

"There is no one here," she said and hung up because she could not delay any longer. She went down to the basement.

The dank air, or the sight of the lock on the door, made her feel taut. She held the scarf so it stretched tight over her head and came to a point where her hand held it. In the dim light of the basement she could have been any woman; she looked like any woman suddenly fearful and alone. So she made no sound when she heard the voice.

". . . because he's as good as dead," said the voice.

She stood by the closed door and listened to Joe's hard laugh.

"Never act like it's done," she heard Bantam say, "until the time. Not before eleven."

"Relax, Bantam. If those guys know what they're doing, it's as good as done."

"Not till eleven. All that's happened is I made a phone call. All that's happened is they got their instructions and now they wait. Now we wait."

Joe said more, and then maybe Bantam said more, but Martha wouldn't have known even had she stayed. The sun wasn't down yet, but once it was, and then eleven o'clock, there would be Charley's death.

They didn't know where he was in the *osteria* and the man in the yard only knew that Charley had taken the Bugatti. There was no one else to ask.

No one knew on the street or on the square, but they had seen the Bugatti. He had driven to town. She would take the short cut over the old bridge. When she came out again, further down where the houses started, she recognized the street he must have taken by car, and she saw the gas station. Sometimes Charley had stopped there to fill up. No, they didn't know, but he had gotten some gas and they told her he had gone into town. The quay, he had said. What part of the harbor? Any one of the quays—

It took her an hour. She had run most of the way and then she had taken a streetcar, the wrong one. The sun was red over the bay and Martha had nowhere to start, everywhere to look. She had cried at first, and asking from place to place her sobbing had become like a dry cough. When the sun was half gone she had covered her small, ridiculous stretch of the waterfront and was going on with miles more curving ahead of her around the bay. She had stopped crying and the only thing that kept her from feeling dead was that Charley was still alive, that there was more to go, that she had to find him.

It might have taken all night had she kept it up. Or maybe all of the next day. She stopped when it had been dark for a while and most of the quays were deserted except for the tourists.

She walked back into the city. It took her longer this time because it was uphill. She walked, saving her strength, no longer frantic, and the calm on her face might have been indifference or determination, or it might have been that there was no strength to make any particular kind of expression. She never slowed down when she went up the steps. Twelve one way, thirteen the other. A piece of wild garden, the kitchen door open, a yellow light on the bare kitchen table. Only Francesca was there. Martha stopped at the table and asked her.

"Where is Joe?" she said.

Chapter Twenty-one

HE HEARD MARTHA the first time, but made no sound on the bed. He lay very still, almost as if he didn't care what went on in the kitchen, and he listened to the two women until it sounded as if Martha might leave. Then he got off the bed and opened the door.

When Martha turned he had to look at her face. It was very white, and her large eyes had the black shine of onyx. Then her scarf slipped off her head.

"Where is Charley?" she said, and though he couldn't have known why she asked the question it made him wary.

"Joe, you must tell me. Joe—"

"You're all worked up," he said. "How about some *aranciata?*"

She reminded him of the other time, turned to stone. He rubbed his palms up and down the sides of his pants. He kept that up, feeling them prickle, the feel that wanted him to ball his hands and make fists. He had a crazy thought that he might hit her, anywhere, but she was stone and the skin would crack over his knuckles. Joe wasn't the kind to have thoughts like that and it made him feel mean.

"Or beer. You know I drink beer. Comes in a can, though."

Then she stood close to him and he didn't remember that she had moved. Her voice was low. It penetrated as if she were screaming.

"By all that is holy to you, Joe, you must answer my question. Please, Joe, even though you might hate me, tell me now where Charley is. This one act in your life will make you good, no matter what else you are. Stop him, Joe, stop them and tell me where Charley—"

"What are you talking about?" he said and went past her to the hearth.

"Joe. I heard Bantam and you in the basement."

He had guessed that she might have, so he wasn't surprised. And it was so much better this way, her knowing what was going to happen at eleven o'clock. Almost an-

114

other hour and a half. He picked up a scallion from the basket by the hearth and bit into it. The sound was as if he had spat at her.

"What basement?" he said.

"Oh, dear Lord—" she said because she saw no way out, only Joe enjoying the game and chewing, slow and with a crunch.

"You mean about that eleven o'clock deal, I guess."

Her voice rang like a blow on steel. "Murdering Charley, I mean. Joe, I have never begged as—"

"So don't start," he said and picked up another scallion.

She went back to the table, and if she hadn't looked so straight it might have been a move to support herself. One hand went down flat on the table and she held her scarf with the other. It almost looked as if her fingers just rested there.

"And I have never threatened," she said. "Stop this now, Joe, or I go to the *carabinièri*."

"With what?"

"To tell them you are murdering Charley, tonight, at eleven o'clock."

"Yeah? Where? You gonna show them where?"

"I will tell them enough so they will kill you."

"I know," he said. He tossed the end of the scallion under the sink, watching it land. "You can do that," he said, "after he's dead."

It was true, and it showed in her face. Joe started to laugh, head back, and it seemed the rock would never stop bouncing. "After he's dead," he kept guffawing, "after he's dead—" when he stopped suddenly and talked normal.

"Unless I get to a phone by ten-thirty, at least."

The switch confused her and she repeated, "Ten-thirty? A phone by ten-thirty—"

"Yeah. It's a quarter to ten now."

"You have—you have forty-five—"

"No, kid," he said. "Not me. *You* have," and he sucked his teeth.

She closed her eyes so she wouldn't see him for a moment, and she listened to the sound of the blood in her throat. It made regular thumps, so regular that she wondered about it. The sound was so calm that she wondered whether this body were her own. Her body did not know what she knew.

"What do you want, Joe?"

"One guess."

"And you will make the call so Charley lives."

"Afterwards."

"Before the forty-five minutes—"

"I work fast. Hey, Fanny," he said, "tell Martha how—"

"Don't make her say anything!"

Joe shrugged and kept watching her. He said, "Well?"

"Of course, Joe," she said.

He kept watching her, wondering if she might cry, or look mean, or maybe try playing her games, but now she looked almost asleep.

"Now, Joe?" She swung the scarf off her shoulder.

"That's what I meant."

"Bring the light," she said. "I cannot see the bed."

"Never mind."

It made her turn back before getting halfway to the door.

"And stop with the buttons," he said. "Keep it on. I know what you look like."

"Joe—"

"You're in a hurry, aren't you?" He nodded at the pine table. "We'll do it here."

She almost broke then, but Joe never saw it. She was like stone when she went to the table and he told her to lean. He told Francesca to take the lamp off the table and hold it, and when the edge of the wood touched Martha's legs from behind she put back her arms, hands on the table.

Her body was not her own, and later she heard Joe say, "It's just after ten." She remembered that he left and that she heard his steps going down to the street. She remembered leaving herself, going through the weeds in the garden.

Chapter Twenty-two

At TEN-FIFTEEN, Joe had gone to the *osteria*. That's where the phone was. He had thought maybe Martha would follow him, but she never did. He drank beer and looked for her to come through the door, to check if he had really called, but she didn't come.

At ten-thirty the two men who had sailed the yawl *Lucrecia* into the Capri harbor left the restaurant near the docks, because it would take them half an hour to get the ship ready the way it had been arranged. They had received their last phone call and ten-thirty was the time for them to leave.

At ten-forty-five the small speedboat made its first arc through the periphery of the harbor. It was an unassuming boat, with no cabin, open in back, just a short canopy with a spray shield, where Charley stood at the wheel. But the motor had a sweet sound. On his second sweep he foamed close to the rim of light where the pilothouse sat on the dock, and when it looked as if the boat would churn right into the pilings Charley throttled all the way back, making the boat squash flat into the water. He sidled her up to the mooring smooth as silk, and kept the motor running.

"*Olà!*" said the old man in front of the pilothouse. "Are you the one from the Susa Company?"

"The same!" Charley secured his boat, jumped back into the rear, and came up again with a box marked Susa Company, Pier 29, Naples. It also said, "Authorized dealers for marine parts Alfa Romeo, Chrysler, Pratt Whitney, Fiat."

"You took your time," said the old man. He watched Charley come up the gangplank and scratched his head. Then he put the sailor cap back on with the button that showed he worked for the harbor master.

"You know how it is, grandfather. Those rich they have no respect for the poor. They break their expensive playthings, and immediately, in the middle of the night, they lift the telephone and summon the poor to fix them." Charley wiped salt spray from his cheek. "But the shop was closed and the boy who delivers could not be found.

117

I think he has a young girl someplace, grandfather, and—
but as I was saying, they got me to bring it." Charley
shrugged. "Of course, I was just there reading the paper,
you understand—"

"I know how it is," said the old man. "You brought the
things for the repair?"

"It's all here. Lift how heavy."

The old man lifted.

"I thought all they needed was a small but important
gasket."

"Of course, grandfather. But I also brought a little
valve, an expensive carburetor, and a pump. Or did you
think I came all the way across from Naples just to sell
them a gasket!"

"Serves them right," said the old man. "They have a
sailboat but they will not sail it as long as the motor
does not run. It serves them right."

"Where is the boat?" said Charley, and looked over the
water.

"You see the one with the sail flapping? Her name is
Lucrecia. They keep it flapping much longer and she will
pull herself free. Real sailors, those rich ones. Serves them
right."

Charley said, *"Addio,"* and went back down the plank,
to his boat. He dropped the box in the back, cast off,
and jumped behind the wheel. He fed the big motor
slowly because he had to wind past moored boats, out to
the spot where the *Lucrecia* was. There would now be
nothing strange about the motor launch making fast next
to the sailboat, and a Susa mechanic boarding in the middle of the night to make an emergency repair. Then they
would drift out to test the motor and shortly afterwards
the mechanic with his box marked Susa Company would
again take off toward Naples.

It was eleven o'clock.

They were both on deck. Since the auxiliary motor was
not supposed to be working, there were no lights on the
Lucrecia. Charley saw they were both tanned, but neither
of them was Italian. Sardinian, perhaps, judging by their
accents. They said, "You are late. Did you bring the box?"

"The old man sent me."

"Did he say to repair our motor?"

"No. He said to repair your valves."

"Come aboard," they said and sounded less formal.

They had exchanged the passwords, and now came the
maneuver with the boats. One of them secured Charley's
launch bow and stern and the other one took Charley's
box. He had a narrow, dark mustache that seemed to
make his mouth twice as wide. The other one was just a
kid. He carried a knife in his belt. While they untied
the mooring rope Charley watched from the stairs that
went down to the cabin. They worked silently, with no
wasted motion, and when the yawl had cast off, the one
with the mustache turned the boat leeward. The *Lucrecia*
started to lean, then move.

Charley went into the small cabin and waited. The
young one came down carrying the box, and took it forward where the door led to the engine compartment. He
came back and closed the blinds over the portholes. Then
he struck a match and lit an oil lamp that hung on the
wall. After that he sat down. He sat on one bunk, Charley
sat opposite. They sat and listened to the water under the
hull and the rope noises from above. Once the kid shifted
because his knife was in the way. Charley took out a pill
and chewed it. They waited like that until the water
started to slap hard against the hull, which meant they
had cleared the harbor. Now they would turn on the motor
so it would sound like testing.

The kid got up, crawled into the forward compartment,
and started the motor. It coughed nicely, went high and
low, but it was not loud enough to cover the other sound.
Charley didn't have to go topside to check and make sure;
there was no other sound like it. The man who had been
at the wheel was furling the sail.

When the kid came back the sail had stopped snapping
and clattering as it slid down the mast. The kid even came
back carrying the duplicate box which held the ampules.
That made it all look right as rain, only the waves were
slapping the other side of the hull now. Had the sail been
up they couldn't have done it that easily. The yawl was
heading out to sea.

Charley got up slowly, and his smile was calm. The
kid saw it, but leaned into the bunk to set the box down,
because everything was right as rain and it was better to
be out a little bit further.

Charley too thought it was okay, but right now, not
much later. His stiff hand went after the kid's kidney
like spearing a potato.

It was all right, except after the first gasp the kid
would gather air and scream with the pain. That's how it
was with kidneys, so Charley went after him again. One
hand yanked at the belt to clear the kid out of the bunk
and the other was ready to slice him in the back of the
neck. Only the kid hit his head coming out of the bunk
and Charley missed. It hurt clipping him on the bone of
the head, and worse, it did no damage.

The kid flung sideways, came free, and when he fell
to the floor rolled on his back. He would have had the
knife out if his kidney wasn't bothering him, and lying
on his back made it worse. His face was screwed up with
the pain and a harsh scream pressed out. If the one at
the wheel had heard it— But the kid's foot caught Charley
in the chest. Not much of a kick, but it made Charley do
the wrong thing, grab the foot, never remembering that
no arm is as strong as a leg.

He remembered when the foot kicked out of his hands
and came up to cut the side of his head. He remembered
there had been enough time for the kid to get at his knife,
pain or no pain, and Charley dropped to the floor without
waiting to see what next. The kid had scrambled around,
and the bare knife was pointing long and sharp out of his
hand. He held it like an expert, not to throw but ready to
slice; not like Joe had but low and weaving back and forth,
the way a snake feels the air before the strike.

It didn't worry Charley, because first the kid had to get
close. He had to get up on his feet, half in a crouch, and
then get Charley in a corner. Charley was going to let
him come and counted on the fact that the kid wasn't apt
to make a sudden move, not with the pain freezing his
muscles. It was good figuring, but suddenly the door flew
open close behind him, the cold sea air raked over the
back of his head, and Charley whirled around. There was
nothing; the door had flown open and the guy at the
wheel was still at the wheel. And the kid was all over
him.

The first slash tore his coat the whole length of the
back; the second one came close to taking off his ear.
But now the kid was much too close, which is no good
with a knife and a busted kidney. This time the kid
screamed good and loud; his legs gave way when Charley
punched him where the ribs come close together, and that's
when Charley had the knife. He had the knife, he held

the sagging kid in front of him, and that's how he was looking straight at the guy who was in the door now.

He must have lashed the wheel, because the yawl kept
on course, and so did the guy in the door. His pencil
mustache seemed to stretch from ear to ear, his teeth
showed big and white, and his hands were big. One was
a fist, the other held a stick.

"One more step, angel face, and your friend gets the
shaft." Charley showed how, holding the knife point close
under the kid's jaw.

Angel face came closer.

"Like this," said Charley and started the knife.

It panicked the kid even though he was practically out
and Charley had a time holding him. But angel face only
came closer. He'd come closer whether the kid was dead
or alive; one more step and the club would come up and
then down, hitting the kid or Charley, not caring who
got it first.

Throwing the knife would do. Charley kept holding the
kid, almost all dead weight now, and tested the arc. He'd
throw underhand, right past the kid's side and going up
as long as there was still room, as soon as the club came,
if the guy meant to lift it. He did. He hauled out, reaching high, the way a tennis player gets set for a serve.
The knife made only half a turn, that's how close they
were, and then Charley saw where it dug into the muscle,
under the guy's arm. He was blue in the face but meant
to finish the swing, which came down in a crazy sweep,
not very accurate, but so hard that it made a dull, no-
bounce crack on the kid's head when Charley pushed
free. The kid clattered down, and then the other one.
He hadn't started to howl yet, only the club had dropped
from his hand. He started to reach for the knife when
Charley jumped over both of them, and while he was going up the steps the screaming started. Charley kept going.

He went for the wheel, unhooked it, then lashed it
again so the yawl started circling with the motor launch
on the outside of the curve. Charley's hands were fluttery
when he untied the lines on his boat. He kept listening
for a sound from the steps, knowing that at least one of
the two down there was able to walk, if he tried hard
enough. Charley tied the bowline again and went downstairs. The kid was out, but angel face sat on the floor,
sweating, trying to get up enough nerve to pull out the

knife. The drug carton was in the left bunk and Charley wanted it. He stepped a little closer to the guy with the knife under his arm and kicked him in the head. The guy lay down quietly and Charley got his box.

But the kick had done the wrong thing. Charley was halfway up the stairs when the guy scrambled up, mad as a bull, yanked the knife out, and fell down again. Nobody pulls a knife out of his own meat without getting faint, and Charley heard the man fall. He barely looked back, held his box tight, and dashed for the gunwale. He unlashed the bowline and jumped into the launch.

He should have taken more time. When the motor kicked over and the launch started to draw away, Charley didn't notice at first how the bowline re-tied itself. But the launch made a sudden jolt, veered hard, and slammed back into the side of the yawl. It couldn't have happened better for the guy with the mustache, because now the launch was in close, and Charley was throwing the clutch while the guy jumped. If he hadn't been roaring to give himself strength he might have got there faster. He might have landed flatfooted instead of catching Charley's punch while in midair, adding his own weight to the thrust, and his jump turning into a thud.

They rolled from one side of the launch to the other while one of them kept roaring and the other grunted with the sheer effort of trying to kill. Then Charley caught himself in time. It couldn't have been worse, after all the preparing and making the maneuver look normal to the old man who watched the Capri harbor. He would remember the yawl waiting there for repairs and Charley coming late at night with engine replacements, and then the next thing the yawl circling aimlessly under the Capri cliffs, running into the rocks, maybe, with the motor intact, the engine replacements still in their box on the cabin floor, a dead man aboard and the other one almost dead.

"Can you hear me?" said Charley and shook the man by the throat. "Can you hear?"

He did. He cursed fluently, as if his tongue wasn't cut, his lips were normal size, and as if he didn't know he had almost been dead.

"Listen. I'm putting you back aboard. I'm hoisting your sail and then I watch you taking her around the island and back to the coast. You hear?"

"I hear."

"Keep going till you make port, the same place where you left. And tell Bantam you delivered the way you were supposed to."

Charley brought the launch close and held on to the side of the sailboat while he watched the man crawl up. He switched off the motor, turned into the wind and got the mainsail up. Then he cast off, making sure it was right this time.

"Keep your split nose close to the wind, Captain Kidd," he yelled, but the guy didn't get it.

Charley watched the yawl heel and take a close, steady course. He was sure the guy at the wheel was a Sardinian. They can handle a ship when they're half dead.

Chapter Twenty-three

SHE HAD TO CLOSE HER EYES when the sun came over the hill, because the sharp light glinted through the leaves outside the window and made a splash on the pillow. She turned slowly and faced the wall. Her clothes were wrinkled and her hair was flattened in back where she had been lying on it. But the wall was too close. The whitewash had grains and cracks which hurt her eyes. Then she got up. She sat on the bed for a while and looked at her hands. They curled as if they were trying to sleep.

She would have to tell Charley. That's what all this was about—Charley alive and coming back. Nothing else really mattered.

When she stood in the kitchen she saw the gun on the table, but she was looking for a glass. She found a glass, drew water at the sink, and drank. She put the glass down and saw the gun again. She picked it up and almost laughed. Then she let it drop on a chair. She should wash, perhaps; she should comb her hair and change. The weeds rustled outside the window and she looked out to see if it was the wind. It was the wind. She filled the glass again and drank a little more water.

It was a good thing she hadn't heard anything sooner, because this way the door opened, he walked in, and she never had time to make a mistake and think it was Charley. Joe closed the door again and nodded at her.

"You look a mess," he said.

She finished drinking water.

"You better leave," she said. "He will be back soon."

He grinned but didn't say anything right away. He saw that she believed what she had said.

"He isn't going to like your looking messy like that. Aren't you changing or something?"

She ran water into a pan and took soap. "I want you to leave now," she said. "I'm going to wash."

"What's the matter? We don't know each other good enough?"

"Of course we do." She found a cigarette, lit it. She

124

thought she would smoke that first and by then he would leave. "Watching me wash won't make you know me any better," she said.

Joe sat down at the table.

"You're a cold one," he said. "To look at you I never figured you'd take a lot of stoking."

She came around to his side of the table and half sat on top of it.

"Joe," she said. "Go away, will you?"

"Afraid I'm going to rape you?"

She exhaled smoke and got up.

"You know you can't rape me," she said and went back to the sink.

He didn't know which way she meant that and Martha didn't seem to care whether he did or not. It made him feel mean. He remembered why he had come and now he was going to do it.

"I was going to tell you about Charley," he said and watched her turn around slowly. "He's okay," he said; "he'll be back." He grinned at her and waited for her to show some expression. "He'll be back," he said again, "but not today."

"When?"

"I was down at the phone," he said. "They got me out of bed to answer it. He called from Capri saying he's on his way to Amalfi on business, and would come back to-morrow noon." When she made no move of any sort he kept talking. "You see? He's safe all this time, he's never even been out of the bay, and tomorrow he'll be back. I kept my end of the bargain."

"I am glad for you," she said.

"So how about keeping yours?"

This time she did show expression. She frowned at him and folded her arms.

"What did you say?"

"Your end of the bargain."

"Joe—" and when she laughed Joe had to look at her to tell what the sound meant— "don't you remember? Last night, Joe. You had your bargain on the table."

"That was no bargain," he said.

"At your price, you can expect no more."

"Christ," he said, but then he started to grin again. "Look, Martha, he won't be back till tomorrow."

"Time to wash off the filth."

"Talk tough if you want. But a bargain's a bargain."

"I have kept mine."

"Like hell. I forced you."

If she hadn't been so surprised she might have laughed again, the way she had done before.

"You know," he said, "you got to do it right. There's a difference."

"Not with you," she said.

"Look. Don't put on. If there's one thing I know, kid—"

"—it is women," she finished for him and killed the cigarette in a drop of water that hung from the faucet.

"I was going to say hoors," he said, but she wasn't paying attention. She watched the wetness soak into the dead stub in her hand and felt very tired. He would keep talking for hours. He might go away and come back later, because he never rushed. Like a slow disease he would stay and stay, never violent but never gone—she would have to tell Charley, or the disease could hang on till the end.

"So?" He sat and waited.

"Joe. Go away."

He took a breath and sounded different.

"I was gonna be nice about it. What's the harm? But remember this, kid—I still got time, same as yesterday, and maybe he won't come back tomorrow."

"You swine! You wouldn't—" But the sudden anger never quite made it and she let it die. Of course he would, he would do the same thing twice, three times, as many times as Charley wasn't there and until he came back. She looked at him so even Joe felt the disgust.

"You wanna try and find out if I'm bluffing?"

She only lowered her eyes.

"That's the spirit. What the hell?" He got up. "What's it to you, after yesterday."

She even thought he might be right. She was so tired, feeling so dull, she hardly bothered to think at all.

"In style," he said. "Get into bed."

She walked into the next room and undressed automatically; shoes, skirt, blouse. Afterwards she lay there and didn't care about covering herself. She heard him go into the kitchen, work the pump. She heard the way he drank.

"Hey, kid," he called. "Get up. Put some clothes on."

She didn't.

"Come on. I don't like my women to walk around naked outdoors."

She sat up because she didn't understand.

"Adele's gone. Yesterday, already. Fanny'll show you where to put your things."

For the first time since the night before she felt herself coming alive, like under a whip.

"Now," he said. "Or maybe you think I'm going to walk back and forth through these weeds every time?"

"What are you saying?"

"You're moving in, I'm saying."

"What are you saying, Joe?"

She walked towards him, straight, and the sight made him feel vicious.

"Stop the clowning, huh? You think you're so good you can come around here and—"

"Answer me!"

"I'll give you an answer, you bitch! From now on you do as you're told, you hold still, and you quit crapping around with your lousy moods. You're moving in, so you learn to act like Fanny, and fast. Or you got an idea Charley's gonna set it all your way again, sister? Wake up. He's been fish bait since midnight!"

"You lie!"

"Come here!" he yelled, and swatted one hand at her.

He thought she was stooping to avoid his hand, and she thought he might follow up and step closer, so she reached the chair fast. Charley had said the closer the better. She fired.

The gun made a jolt, something she hadn't known about, but then Joe started to swivel, and when his head hit the sink Martha's thought was that the pain would make him more angry.

When she saw the blood soak up where the belt came around his waist it caught up with her. She gasped, then she suddenly screamed. She screamed with the pressure of all that had gone wrong and all that could never be right.

She put her hands around herself because she felt naked. It was the only thing that didn't confuse her, so she went into the other room and put on her clothes. Then she walked out through the kitchen where the gun was on the floor, and where Joe was. He could almost reach it. She didn't see that he tried because she was only thinking of what didn't confuse her. The simplest thing was to walk, so she walked through the weeds and down the thirteen steps one way and twelve the other.

Chapter Twenty-four

CHARLEY DELMONT held the wheel with the left hand because it hurt his knuckles to hold on with the right one. It made him drive the Bugatti in jerks, because when the streets got narrower and twisted through Pizzofalcone he wouldn't slow down. Then he saw the *carabinièri* come down the sidewalk. There was never one, they always walked in twosomes. Charley slowed down when he saw them. It was a habit.

He held himself back all the way up the hill and through the outskirts where the *osteria* was, but when he pulled into the yard the back wheels skidded and dug two black lines into the dirt. He bucked it to a stop and jumped out. He didn't forget to carry the carton into the basement. He came back at a jog and kept it up all the way to the stairs. He stopped to look at them for a second, patted his side where the knife was, and went up.

He met no one. And the kitchen was empty.

The main thing now was to keep his head. The main thing was to fix that bastard for good but not altogether, not before they had their talk.

He had the knife out and kicked open the door. He waited for Francesca to turn around. She had been folding shirts on the dresser and didn't know about Joe, but he ought to be back by now. He hadn't even taken his glass of milk in the morning.

Charley went back to the kitchen and looked at the glass of milk on the table. He squinted into the bright sun outside, across the weeds. They moved, but it wasn't the wind.

Charley almost fell over Joe, crawling there like a dog, his face a bad color and the shirt all stained. He ran across to his house, with the knife still in his hand. The house was empty, but the gun made him sure. One shot, just the way he would have done it—but it couldn't have been very close because the bleeding pig was still alive. One shot to scare him off, and hitting him into the bargain. She must have been scared and ran.

128

Thinking of Joe he started to curse all the way back through the weeds. He'd saved his temper all the way over from Capri, and now there was nothing he could do with it. He watched Joe crawl through the grass, and watching him made Charley break out in a sweat. It ran down his back and itched in his palms, but Charley walked very slowly because Joe was setting a slow pace. Charley followed him into the kitchen still holding the knife.

Joe pulled himself up by the table and looked beat. The two men looked at each other and Joe was licking his lips.

"Chuck. I'm hit."

"Don't talk. Just get better fast, you sonofabitch. I'll be waiting."

Francesca had rushed over. She held one of Joe's arms but didn't know what to do.

"My side, Chuck, I think it's still in there. Chuck—"

Charley put the knife away and started to smile.

"To do it up brown you ought to come up the stairs first. You should—"

"Chuck, dammit, I still got the slug. Take it out before the thing starts rotting on me."

"Joe, I wouldn't want to miss it. Get on the table."

Joe stretched out. The tip of his nose looked white, and his eyes had the wide-open meanness of a weasel. Charley came back with the box of instruments and the medicinal bottles.

"Take off his pants, Fanny."

She did and looked at the wound. There was a hole in front and a gash in back, clean path through the meat over his hip.

"Let me tell you," said Charley, "I'm disappointed. It came out whole."

Joe just cursed under his breath.

"I'll clean it out," said Charley and poured alcohol into a dish. He washed his hands in it and poured the stuff out. Then he filled the dish again.

"Want a shot?"

"Yeah. Gimme."

Charley gave him the bottle. The stuff was pure ethyl without anything else.

"I hope it eats your insides," he said.

Joe drank and turned blue. When he relaxed again Charley got ready with a swab.

"Where's Martha?"

Joe burped, but that was when the swab went in and he almost convulsed himself off the table. Charley pulled the swab out and threw it away.

"Where's Martha."

"Christ," said Joe. He was panting.

Charley did a neat job because he wanted Joe to live. Then he told Joe to roll on his stomach because he wanted to sew the gash where the bullet had torn out.

"Before I trim, where's Martha?"

"She ran off. Honest to God, Chuck, get this thing over with—"

Charley started to trim with the surgical scissors and Joe held on to the table to keep from jumping off.

"She all right, Joe?"

Joe had started to tremble.

"Answer me."

"She's all right, she's all right—"

Charley tore open a suture pack and started to sew. He did a nice even job, working fast, and Joe never went under. When the bandage was on Joe slumped on his back.

"Another shot?"

Joe lay there too exhausted to answer. Charley packed away the things and Francesca picked up the soiled stuff. She got a bucket of water, a stiff brush and soap and went for the table top next to Joe. When he saw her he hauled out with one arm but missed because she was bending low to do her scrubbing.

"Scrub later," said Charley, "or he'll start using that filthy language again."

She went to sit on the hearth and every so often she looked over at the table top.

"You want to lie in bed?" said Charley.

"Never mind. Just let me get my breath."

Joe stayed on the table, and they heard how his breathing got better. After a while his hands came to lie at his side. They were no longer white-knuckled like at first, nor limp and useless. They were like always, big and resting there.

"It's been maybe an hour," said Charley. "Where's Martha?"

Joe turned his head and saw Charley sitting in the chair. The smile was back on his mouth. He sat quietly and then

Joe saw he was holding a bottle. He hadn't put the alcohol back.

"Chuck—you been drinking that?"

"She better show up soon, Joey, or I'm going to worry. And you better worry, Joe."

Charley uncorked the bottle and took a slow drink.

"Christ, Chuck—"

"Yes, Joey?"

"Chuck, listen to me. You know better than drinking that stuff, you know—"

"Shut up, Joey," and it sounded unconcerned.

The first thing she recognized after walking and walking was the back yard where the car was, behind the *osteria*. She didn't wonder how she had gotten there because once she started to think again it was about Joe on the floor. She didn't think about Charley, she hadn't thought about that since the shot. Now, walking past the yard, she saw the Bugatti and still couldn't think about Charley. But she had stopped. She stared at it without moving and then she started to run.

Charley put down the bottle and then put his hands behind his head.

"Why did she take that shot at you, Joey? Tell it again."

"A hundred times, Chuck, I've told you a hundred times and you wouldn't listen—"

"So tell it again. Tell it again so you know why you're going to be dead. And stay where you are, Joe." Charley smiled. He reached down for the bottle. "If I were religious, Joe, I'd ask Fanny to bring out two candles. Or is it four? I think they use four and put them at the corners—"

Charley dropped the bottle, and it broke. He saw Martha, and jumped up. They didn't talk; they only held each other.

Joe lay still on the table and waited. He wasn't impatient and he wasn't afraid any more. He was like a very primitive animal that can't be destroyed. He watched them come apart and made his move.

"Martha," he said. "The bargain. I kept my bargain."

Chapter Twenty-five

To CHARLEY, Martha had come back from a walk. To Martha, Charley had come back from the dead.

She kept her hand on his arm, and when Joe talked it was just a voice. For a moment nothing could matter to her except that Charley's arm was under her hand, and she felt it warm and moving.

"You want to lie down for a while?" said Charley. "Martha, look at me—"

She looked at him and shook her head. "It's all right now," she said. "You're back."

"Sure, honey, I'm back." He patted her shoulder and put his hand in her hair. "If you're all right—"

She said, "I'm all right," but now all the rest was back too, the bargain, the weakness, and the evil secrecy which was as bad as the truth. She looked at Joe's face and saw the bland eyes and the mouth smiling.

"Tell me about it," said Charley. "Tell me how bad it was."

That's when Joe started to laugh. "Bad!" and he only stopped laughing because it hurt his side. "Tell him how good it was, kid! So go ahead, tell him!"

Charley got very still and when he talked his mouth hardly moved.

"Martha. Shall I kill him?"

"You want her to break up?" But the way Joe said it there was hardly a question in it. "You want to make her stupid brains work overtime dreaming up a good one to match your stupid question? Listen to me, you dumb jerk, and you better sit down so your rear don't drag when you hear this."

"Keep it up, Joe."

"You're damn right I'm keeping it up. That hoor's caused enough trouble around here."

"I don't care how shot up you are," said Charley and whipped Joe across the face.

But it hardly made a pause. Joe was getting faster because he had to get it all in before Charley stopped listening.

"You see Adele around here?" he yelled. "You wanna ask Fanny what happened to Adele? She's gone, I sent her away. Tell him, Fanny, did I send her packing?"

Francesca nodded. She was holding the scrub brush in her hand and stood waiting by the hearth.

"I had to send her away right after you left. You know why, jerk? Because your roommate there, she comes waving in here with a gun. You have to give her a gun, you jerk, so she can bulldoze her way into here. If you don't send them away, she says, I'll kill myself. Joe baby, she says—"

Charley did it again. His flat hand made a hard sound across Joe's face, but it stopped nothing.

"I want you, she says. And waving that gun there I don't argue. With your roommate standing right there I send Adele packing, but quick. That, you jerk, is the short version of one long argument. And next. You know what comes next?"

"What comes next, Joe?"

"I go to her house with her—the gun, you know. And if you didn't guess it by now—"

Charley looked over to Martha, but she had her eyes closed. She was standing that way, waiting for Joe to finish and waiting for Charley to end the nightmare.

"Maybe you think I'm out of my head?" Joe was roaring. He swung out one arm and caught Martha by the short sleeve of her blouse. There was a rip. "Take a look at that, you stupid sap, take a look at the way she bruises!"

There was a dark mark on her shoulder where the blouse had come off.

"And don't tell me that you did that!" He watched Charley and when he saw Charley starting to smirk and his hand go up to his belt, Joe added the next thing, slowly, "How do you think I did it, sap? With this bullet in my gut?" Charley stopped to listen. "You gotta be healthy to do right by her. She shot me afterwards. When I said it was the last time." Then Joe waited to see how it worked.

It was a fine story, and Martha's bruise showed on her bare shoulder so Charley could look at it. He looked at her and waited for her to say something. But to Martha it didn't need words. It needed love and one look between them, and words wouldn't count for much after that. Martha opened her eyes and when she saw Charley she saw the question and the waiting.

All the words wouldn't count for anything.

Her head stayed upright, and she cried with eyes wide open. After a while it racked her and the shaking got so bad she sank to the floor and cried, never stopping all the time while Charley picked her up and carried her back to the house. He felt like wood. He put a blanket over her and left the house.

He went back across the garden. Joe hadn't moved. Francesca was in the next room, lying on the bed, because she had nothing to do. Charley went to close her door, came back to the table. Joe waited. He saw Charley next to him but he couldn't tell anything by the face.

"Tell it again, Joe."

"You don't believe me?"

"Tell it again, Joe. There's time. I'm not going to kill you fast if you play games with me."

Joe started to sweat and tried to rear off the table.

When Charley pushed him back Joe hit the back of his head with a hard thump, but Joe was talking already. It got fast and high while Charley watched him with a face that seemed almost asleep.

"You don't know what she is, Chuck, you picked her up and don't know the first thing about her. Chuck, listen to me, that woman's been nothing but trouble, you know that, Chuck, and you not knowing the half of it about that—about that—"

"Don't say hoor, Joe."

Joe didn't say hoor. The less he saw in Charley's face the more he got afraid. Perhaps repeating the story would be a mistake, perhaps repeating it would give him an idea, another lie to add, another piece of time before Charley broke the hold on himself. And if nothing made a dent there was still the ace in the hole, but Joe wanted to hold it until nothing else seemed to work because the ace in the hole could mean murder for sure, anybody's murder.

"How come she shot you, Joe?"

"I told you, I explained how—"

"It didn't make sense."

"I told you she isn't what you think she is. You never took the trouble—"

Charley didn't want to hear about it. Joe was a liar and Martha— Who was Martha? She'd been on the bridge, and that's all he had ever found out.

"Try this, Joe. How come I was ambushed?"

"Was what?" Joe kept his mouth open.

"Try hard, Joe."

There was some life in Charley's face now, and Joe saw it.

"I never trusted that Bantam, Chuck. You remember the way I felt—" He got a painful clip across the loose mouth but it wasn't serious yet.

"Harder, Joe."

"For chrissakes, Chuck, I'm lying here sick and—"

"Bantam had nothing to gain from it."

Joe frowned, because it was getting out of hand. He gasped when Charley got the knife out, but then Charley tossed it across the room. It stuck in the beam over the hearth and Charley said, "We'll try again, Joe. With the bare hands only. How come—"

He stopped because Martha was back.

She had the shawl over her head and her face was dark. All of her looked dark with the sun behind her, very low now, because the day was almost over.

"Martha—"

"No, Charley. I came to talk. Then I go."

He tried interrupting her once more, but her cold voice stopped him, the voice of a stranger, and when he saw her face closer he was surprised that she didn't look tired any more. She looked cold, and alive with anger.

"So you will know about him," she said. "So when I leave you will know he is not through with you yet."

"Martha, I know—"

"You know nothing." The sharpness was like a slap. She kept it that way so nothing else would show, the defeat, the loss in her life. "He told me you would be dead if I did not give him his way. I overheard him talking— he and the man with the suit—how they meant to kill you, and then Joe wasn't going to stop them from killing you unless I gave in." She talked faster to get it out of the way. "And I let him because what is a small, filthy thing—in order to save you, I thought. So it was a bargain and I had forgotten that you do not win a bargain with the devil, because afterwards he came back and told me that you were dead. And I believed him and shot him for that." She was screaming.

"I thought you could shoot the devil and it would be over. I thought all my evil could buy something good and believed it even more when I saw you back, except I should have known nothing mattered any more." Her voice dropped but she held it in hard, even tones. "After the devil, Charley, even you could not come back. I was not your Martha any more. I saw this because you listened to him and you doubted me. I think you really did have to doubt me, because I was no longer the same. Nothing is," she said, and when she turned and was gone Charley looked at the empty door as if he were waiting to wake up.

He then did the thing that was closest. His hands were around Joe's throat and for a soundless moment nothing else existed except that neck with the muscles thick on each side and the breath caught.

There was a struggle and then almost no time to spare.

"Chuck—hear me—after her, run after—"

Charley pressed harder.

"Delmont—bridge, Delmont—she knows—police—" He let go so suddenly that Joe kept twisting when he was already free. Then he heard Charley's voice, hoarse and full of hate.

"What did you say? I'll kill you in spite—"

"Run, Chuck. She's after you. You and Delmont under the bridge! She saw—" Joe got his breath and his voice turned into a roar. "How else would I know except she told me about it! At first I kept her from using it, but now—"

Charley was gone. His run was a crazy stumble through the weeds and to the house where the Judas tree grew.

She had taken nothing. She was gone, and everything was still there, even the gun on the floor. It looked almost as if she meant to come back. He scooped up the gun and ran back through the weeds, and then down the long steps. He never stumbled. It was quite dark now, and the steep way down could have broken him many times, but nothing stopped him any more. He ran on without anything in the way any more.

Chapter Twenty-six

IF SHE HAD LEFT for good, he knew which way she would go. If she meant to come back she would go the same way, because the *gendarmeria* was in the same direction.

Crossing the square, he turned uphill by habit because he always went uphill to get the car before going down into town. He would lose her with the car. Once she crossed over into Pizzofalcone she could disappear in the tangled streets, through archways and courtways leading into the next alley. Or she could even hole up there, spend the night or days with somebody—for how many lire, for whatever it was worth to her. It had been worth holding it back from him, never talking about the black sight she had seen from the bridge because she probably knew how he would handle that.

She had known all along. She had been so sure in her secret that she even came back for one grandstand play there in the kitchen. Perhaps the police knew already, and that's why she was that sure—but not sure enough not to run that last minute. She knew how he would handle it now.

He ran the other way and knocked over a child in the square. There were couples and old people but they stepped aside and made no noise. Let him run. If he goes away there will be no trouble.

Perhaps she had run, too, and her lead was too great. Charley ran around the corner into the dirt road by the house where the roof had fallen in. But perhaps she was thinking he was busy up in the kitchen. By rights he'd be killing Joe now, and then he'd have Fanny on his hands who'd maybe wake and start screaming. It wasn't far to the alleys beyond the ravine. If she had made it—

There was a spray of gravel when he skidded down to the old bridge and he started to race again. There wasn't enough light to tell the other side clearly, but it was all right not to look that far because she was still on the

137

bridge. The shawl was over her head making a tall, head-less shape, very dark.

To Charley it looked like a monster.

She must have heard because she turned and stopped. And she hadn't been walking fast, he noticed, but slow and sure. She stood and watched him come. He wasn't running any more. He had stopped, drawn the gun, and probing it out ahead of him he had started to walk in a tense crouch. This time it felt right all the way. No sick pain, no doubt, and he started to kill her every step of the way.

Then he stopped, and she didn't move.

"So you saw," he said.

The monster without the head did not move and the voice was without feeling.

"I saw what?"

It felt to him as if he was going to giggle, and it needed some strong impact to keep him sane. He would look at the monster and remember the bridge. He would step closer, look at her, and remember the bridge.

"Charley—" she said, and he could hardly hear. The blindness of his run was wearing off and her voice was Martha's voice again. She had moved her head, a small move, and seeing her face now it was hard to remember the monster. He didn't notice how his gun hand went down.

"Why did you come, Charley?" The voice was weary, but Martha's voice.

"Why did I come?"

"It is too late, Charley."

"Too late? What's too late?" He had to repeat auto-matically just to do something, to become himself again and not go dizzy under a spell she was weaving. Every-thing Joe had said was an evil trick. But the thing under the bridge—Joe hadn't been there; Martha had. With an effort of will, Charley tried thinking. No more feelings now—no more hate feelings for Joe and love feelings for Martha—because they were both blinding spells and once and for all he had to know. He looked away from Mar-tha and focused on something far.

"What did you tell him? What did you tell him about that first night?"

At first she didn't understand, and the emptiness inside her gave her no will. She would have liked to hear nothing and see nothing. His hand was on the stone rail of the bridge, rubbing it with fingers working the stone.

"What did you tell him about the bridge?" The hand worked back and forth.

The bridge again. He had to tear her open again, to push her into remembering. Martha suddenly felt like crying.

"Say it!" His voice pushed.

"Say it?" she repeated. "Say what? Say what, Charley? What is there to say?"

He heard Martha's voice again, tired now, asking him to let her be. It was the spell again that would soon make him forget what he had to find out if he wanted to stop running.

"You leaned over the bridge and saw me. What did you see?"

"Nothing, Charley. It was dark. I was only wondering—"

"Wondering what?"

"Wondering what might be there. I had heard the moan. Nothing else, Charley, please believe me—"

"More. Remember more."

"I can't remember more. Believe me, Charley. I never think—I never thought of the first night when I thought of you, and when we—" Then she could only cry.

It was Martha crying, and Charley could hardly remember the monster. And he would have to run forever, doubt forever if he thought of her now. If it killed her he had to get it out of his life. She would know nothing and tell him so and they would be free—so ask her! Her pain could not be more than his.

He looked away from her, watching his hand.

"You did see; you told me the first time. You saw me walking at first."

"Please, Charley—"

He clamped his hand on the stone to make a pain, a sharp, distracting pain from the palm through the hand and into his arm.

"And you saw me walking! And you saw something else when I walked!"

"What, Charley? What did I see?" Once more she tried not to remember.

"Me and what else? A man? A body?"

The crying was gone; once she remembered, the unbearable fear would be gone. So she shook back her shawl and screamed, "Yes! You and a body. Was the body dead? Ask me! The body was dead. You went to the river with a corpse on your back. Is it right? Do I remember it right?"

"Right as right!" he screamed back, because only a scream would keep him going ahead. The torture could not get worse. "Go on! What next?"

Now she needed no prodding. With her full hair making a shape like the very first time, making Charley remember, she screamed, "—and down the embankment! He was dead. You killed him, and you went down to the bridge. I heard you there with the body, and you must have been stuffing his pockets. They always do. They stuff the pockets on the corpse with stones, and with another stone maybe kill him again to be sure, though you may not have done it. You kill well the first time so he was dead and full of stones and you rolled him over just to check if he was ready, to check if he was heavy enough. More weight. A chain from your car perhaps? It was so dark, but ask me, ask me and I will remember—" She stopped for breath, very suddenly. It was like a jar to Charley.

"Yes, more," he said, without screaming this time because it hardly mattered. "All of it!"

"Oh, all of it, all of it then. You pushed him into the Tiber, slowly to make no splash, but the effort because of his weight made you wince from the wound in your side. Then I heard you moan—like a cat, you said. Then you were there with the gun on me because I had to be killed, except the wound made you weak, something made you weak all this time, did it not? Weak all this time and that's how you gave me time to live a little while longer—"

She was through. She did not even hope he would contradict her, because now she was through.

"You told this to Joe?"

"You care?"

His hand with the raw palm hung by his side and didn't feel like his own any more. The pain didn't feel like his own any more.

"And you went to the police?"

She put the shawl back over her head and took a step. Then she said, "Does it matter?"

"Why did you wait this long?"

"I am going away," she said. "I am going now." Only the simplest thing occurred to her then, and having taken a step she thought of walking.

"You can't," he said.

"You have more to ask?"

"No. You've said everything."

"I have said everything. All you have asked me to say."

They stood like puppets, they had talked like puppets, and then his right arm moved up because that's how the puppet was built. The gun aimed low, a belly target that even a puppet could hit.

But his arm started to tremble. If he could see the monster now—not Martha—standing waiting again.

His voice was suddenly loud. "What else? What else is there, Martha?"

In the silence he saw how she shook her head.

"Martha!"

"It doesn't matter."

"Martha! What?"

"It doesn't matter. You have killed me."

He didn't move for fear he would drop the gun.

"I didn't. I didn't before and if I kill you it is the first time."

"I know. How could I have loved you?"

His gun arm moved and he was aware of his muscles. They felt as if they were seeking sleep.

"I know," she said. "Except you would kill me twice. The second time with a gun."

The gun was a weight, a useless weight, and his hand hung down, as if relaxing.

"I know," he said. "I believe you. I believe everything now."

But he had lost. She didn't come to him, and he didn't expect her to. He didn't move towards her because she had said it right, he had killed her. He watched her raise the shawl, cover her head, and leave. He watched her leave. It seemed from a distance as if they had never known each other.

Chapter Twenty-seven

IT WAS DARK at the end of the bridge where he had seen her last, and only the railing seemed to reach out into the darkness. After a while he put his hand on the railing and felt the stone with his fingers.

He could see the curve of light along the bay, and by turning his head a little he could see Vesuvius. The mountain itself was hard to see in the dark, but a red reflection was pulsing over the crater. The thin cloud over Vesuvius rose straight and still, reflecting the hot lava.

His right hand had started to tingle. He closed the fingers because he did not want to drop the gun. He left the bridge and went up the hill, up the twelve and thirteen steps, through the weeds, to the terrace, and into his house. Joe could wait one moment longer. Charley turned on the light and took a drink from the pump. Then he heard Joe, so he went back to the terrace.

Joe walked with a cane. He came slowly because the weeds were thick and he hurt. When he was close enough he couldn't tell a thing that was different because Charley was looking at him and the mask was back on.

"You come back alone?" Joe craned his neck to see better.

"What do you want?"

Joe didn't answer. He wasn't sure how to start, so he first climbed up on the terrace, grunting. Then his cane thudded closer.

"I saw you from the kitchen."

"That's nice."

Joe stopped close by and his breathing was making a sound. After a while, when Charley still didn't move, he asked, "You took care of her?"

"Why? You come to view the corpse?"

Charley turned and went into the house. He turned by the door that went into the bedroom and waited for Joe. Joe's mouth was open and he stopped by the kitchen table.

"So say something."

"Sure. What?"

"What's the matter, you sore or something?" Charley looked at him and his habit was back. He was smiling.

"You come to view the corpse?"

"I said are you sore or something. You don't see me being sore, and after all that crap you gave me back there!"

"I took yours, you take mine."

"What's that?"

"I said, you take mine."

Then Joe got sore. "You don't think so good, Chuck. I just did you a favor, remember?"

"Sure."

"So what is this, for chrissakes—" Charley's smile was starting to grate on Joe and Joe got meaner. "You got an idea you're going to push me around? After you leave her a gun to cripple me, after that hero stuff slapping me around with me flat on my back, after I put myself out and save your lousy skin for you? Get this, Delmont, we don't go for that lousy moody stuff and that slapping around you do, and that—"

"So?"

"So don't get tough with me, because what she knew I know! And what I know Bantam knows! I got a message for you, Delmont. You don't like running? Well, you better! You think you got a name? Like hell you do, Delmont! You think you killed her to save your skin, you stupid, grinning ass? You killed her because I told you to, because she never saw a damn thing under that bridge, never said a word to me, never crossed you except when I made her do it! That's what you better learn, Delmont, and from now on when I say jump, you jump! Got that clear?"

"That's what she said," said Charley.

And then Joe started to shout because it kept the confusion out and perhaps Charley would break. "So she said it and I said it and now she's dead and I've got you for sure! Make a bargain with the devil, she said; make a bargain and lose. Well, you lost, Chuck boy, and I'm here to tell you—"

"Want to view a corpse?"

"I'm viewing one!" While Joe spoke he took a step and hauled out with his cane.

"You missed, Joey." The smile was gone and Joe saw

the loser turn into something else. Like the devil himself.
"Don't miss again," Charley said.

Joe saw he had gone the limit. He hauled out again
and a bloody gash sprung open on Charley's head. He
didn't see more because the stick yanked him hard and
Charley had stepped aside. Joe got a push from behind,
stumbled, hit hard on the bed in the next room.

Joe saw Charley standing in the doorway, and then
Charley had the gun in his hand.

"Chuck! Chuck, listen—"

"You came to view a corpse, Lenken—"

"Chuck, you got a gun. Chuck, I can't even move, I'm
sick! I can't—"

"—die even," said Charley and tossed the gun on the
bed.

Joe could be fast. He was firing before the gun was
up and he thought he was still firing when the cane
smashed his wrist, then his nose.

Charley was through then. He dropped the cane and
turned away without caring to look. Joe made a stain on
the bed.

Charley walked around the Judas tree so he could see
the view. The bay was one way, and to the side was
Vesuvius. The thin cloud over Vesuvius seemed to stand
still, and it looked white. Charley went down the steps,
first one way, then the other. He crossed the square and
went down where the bridge was. Where Martha had
been. He went to the place where he had seen her last.

THE END
of a novel by
Peter Rabe

www.ingramcontent.com/pod-product-compliance
Lightning Source LLC
Chambersburg PA
CBHW022025170626
46808CB00003B/1063